Dear Reader,

I celebrate twenty years  just as Harlequin's Ame celebrates twenty years you. So how appropria *That Summer in Maine*, American Romance's 20th Anniversary Celebration.

I feel a particular devotion to the line because of its promise to produce books about heart, home and happiness, because—given those ingredients— anything is possible. My life is a case in point.

My mother died when I was four months old, and her sister and brother-in-law extended themselves to give me a home.

In Los Angeles, a city of millions, the one man in the world who could understand my need for kids, cats and chocolate found me and offered me his heart.

And when infertility threatened to deprive us of the children we wanted, we found three of them anyway—and all at once! Happiness!

Everything you want is out there—you just have to believe in love. And read Harlequin American Romance for inspiration.

My best wishes to you!

Muriel Jensen

Dear Reader,

Welcome to another wonderful month at Harlequin American Romance. You'll notice our covers have a brand-new look, but rest assured that we still have the editorial you know and love just inside.

What a lineup we have for you, as reader favorite Muriel Jensen helps us celebrate our 20th Anniversary with her latest release. *That Summer in Maine* is a beautiful tale of a woman who gets an unexpected second chance at love and family with the last man she imagines. And author Sharon Swan pens the fourth title in our ongoing series MILLIONAIRE, MONTANA. You won't believe what motivates ever-feuding neighbors Dev and Amanda to take a hasty trip to the altar in *Four-Karat Fiancée*.

Speaking of weddings, we have two other tales of marriage this month. Darlene Scalera pens the story of a jilted bride on the hunt for her disappearing groom in *May the Best Man Wed*. (Hint: the bride may just be falling for her husband-to-be's brother.) Dianne Castell's *High-Tide Bride* has a runaway bride hiding out in a small town where her attraction to the local sheriff is rising just as fast as the flooding river.

So sit back and enjoy our lovely new look and the always-quality novels we have to offer you this—and every—month at Harlequin American Romance.

Best Wishes,

Melissa Jeglinski
Associate Senior Editor
Harlequin American Romance

MURIEL JENSEN
That Summer in Maine

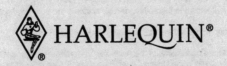

HARLEQUIN®

TORONTO • NEW YORK • LONDON
AMSTERDAM • PARIS • SYDNEY • HAMBURG
STOCKHOLM • ATHENS • TOKYO • MILAN • MADRID
PRAGUE • WARSAW • BUDAPEST • AUCKLAND

To the Dinner Dames: Bobbi, Sunny, Dorothy and Susan

ISBN 0-373-16965-5

THAT SUMMER IN MAINE

Visit us at www.eHarlequin.com

Printed in U.S.A.

ABOUT THE AUTHOR

Muriel Jensen and her husband, Ron, live in Astoria, Oregon, in an old foursquare Victorian at the mouth of the Columbia River. They share their home with a golden retriever/golden Labrador mix named Amber, and five cats who moved in with them without an invitation. (Muriel insists that a plate of Friskies and a bowl of water are *not* an invitation!)

They also have three children and their families in their lives—a veritable crowd of the most interesting people and children. In addition, they have irreplaceable friends, wonderful neighbors and "a life they know they don't deserve, but love desperately anyway."

Books by Muriel Jensen

HARLEQUIN AMERICAN ROMANCE

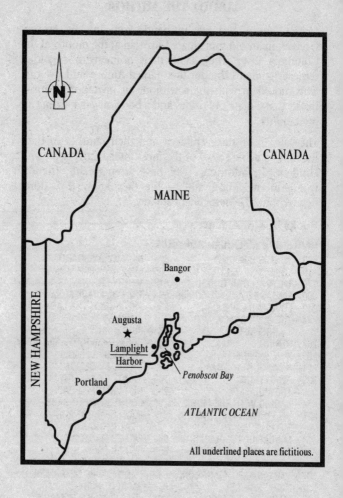

CANADA

CANADA

MAINE

NEW HAMPSHIRE

Bangor
•

Augusta
★

Lamplight
Harbor
•

Penobscot Bay

Portland
•

ATLANTIC OCEAN

All underlined places are fictitious.

Prologue

June 23, 9:53 p.m.
Somewhere in the Pyrenees Mountains

Kidnapped!

Maggie Lawton offered sincere apologies to Robert Louis Stevenson as she assessed her situation. She watched with a weird sort of disassociation as the leader of the Basque separatists who'd ambushed her party of six on a hiking trail in the Parc National des Pyrenees spoke to his small army of men gathered around the campfire. They all wore the red *boina* or beret that was a political statement and a badge of pride for the movement.

To distract herself from the nighttime chill, she remembered that she'd played a kidnapped Arabian princess years ago in her one and only foray into musicals. It had run just fourteen months, and she'd been glad when it was over. Her costume had been skimpy and the theater cold.

She tried to remember the lyrics of the number she

sang when captured by Bedouins and held for ransom. It had been jaunty and heroic and she'd sung it loudly and with broad gestures, hoping her enthusiasm would disguise the fact that she had a poor voice.

"Why, for God's sake, are you humming?" Baldrich Livingston, her costar in several long runs at London's Old Vic, and the grumpiest man in Europe, glowered at her in the light of the campfire. "There's no audience beyond the lights, dear heart, and no intermission in fifteen minutes! This is real! Our pal *le compte* has gotten us into it this time!"

Gerard Armand, Compte de Bastogne, leaned around Glen and Priscilla Thicke to defend himself. Maggie and her companions sat side by side on the cold ground, their wrists tied behind their backs. "Oh, *certainement!* Blame me! Celine and I had plans to go to Monte Carlo for the weekend, but the four of you barge into my villa uninvited!"

Glen, who was Maggie's agent, a practical man in his early fifties, took exception to that. "It was your birthday, Jerry. We came to surprise you and help you celebrate."

"You came," he returned, "because my servants spoil you and you are able to bask in my reflected glory. You theater people have wealth but no style, unless you borrow it from your royal friends!"

Baldy rolled his eyes. "Please don't say bask."

"Yes," Prissie added while adjusting the sleeves of her chic little hiking jacket. "And you know very well you could not have taken your *chère aimée* to

Monte Carlo, Jerry. She may be old enough for your bed, but I'm sure she's far too young to gamble.'' That observation made, Prissie turned her attention to the Basque leader. ''*Monsieur! Monsieur!* May we have water, please? We have been sitting here in the cold for hours! I'd like something sparkling, not still.''

Baldy rolled his eyes again and even Glen said under his breath, ''Priss, shut up.''

She bristled indignantly. ''Why? If they want to hold us for ransom or to make some political point, that's fine. I'm sure the publicity won't hurt. But I don't intend to die of thirst or starvation while we wait for rescue.''

''Do you know nothing?'' Gerard demanded. ''These people are not playing! They are terrorists! Murderers! They would kill us in a heartbeat if—''

''Monsieur le Compte!'' The leader of their kidnappers, a muscular man of average height and considerable presence, paced in front of them, an Uzi hooked over his shoulder. He was handsome, but there was a zealot's fever in his eyes.

Maggie felt a chill trickle down her spine as his gaze touched each one of her companions, rested on her a moment, then focused on Gerard. ''You malign me,'' he said in an amiable tone that was eerie for all its gentleness. ''I fight for my people, though my French Basque brothers are more passive and peaceful than our cousins in Spain, whom I prefer to emulate. We are descendants of the original Iberians and have lived here since before the Celts arrived thirty-five hundred years ago, yet every civilization to live here has preferred to pretend we do not exist. They've pushed us higher and higher into the mountains. I am not a murderer, *monsieur*. I'm simply trying to find a place for my people."

"What do you think we can do for you?" Baldy asked in a voice slightly thinner than his usually commanding center-stage tones.

The man smiled and took several steps to stand in front of Maggie. "Your designer clothes highlight rather than disguise who you are. Maggie Lawton, American-born star of the British stage. Baldrich Livingston, son of a Liverpool dockworker, former star of *London Weekend Television* and now Miss Lawton's leading man. Glen and Priscilla Thicke, powerful theatrical agent and his Long Island society wife, and *le compte de Bastogne,* toast of every social affair in Europe, and his lover, the daughter of French businessman Etien Langlois and his fashion designer wife, Chantal."

He paced a little and drew a deep breath.

"I believe the *London Mail* calls you The Wild Bon Vivants because of your penchant for parties."

"One is here," Prissie said, "to have a good time."

The leader nodded. "Here I have had it all wrong," he said, as though her words were a revelation. "I thought we were here to ease the plight of our fellow man."

"And yet your actions," Maggie said, "have increased our plight."

"It will be over soon, *madame*," he said genially. "I have just spoken to your State Department. Either your ransom will bring us a small fortune with which to continue our work, or your deaths will make a strong statement about our dedication to our cause."

Prissie gasped, and Celine began to sob. The men subsided in the face of the grim truth Maggie suspected but hadn't been anxious to say aloud.

The leader raised an eyebrow at Maggie's continued calm.

"You doubt my commitment, Mrs. Lawton?" he asked.

She shook her head. "I do not," she replied, thinking how liberating it was to have no fear of death. For two years she'd carried the burden of having to go on living. But now her fearlessness might finally stand her in good stead. "Early in my career I was in a film about Miguel Angel Blanco." He'd been a Basque politician murdered by ETA, a radical group dedicated to securing a united Basque state.

He nodded. "*Basta Ya.* I saw it." He studied her with sudden intensity. "Was that beautiful blond girl you?"

She had to smile at his sincere surprise. Apparently, the past two years had not been kind to her. "You are no gentleman, sir. That was more than twenty years ago, and my makeup man was not along on this hike."

A subtle change took place in his expression, and

he sat down on a flat rock opposite her. "Yes," he said slowly. "You have had a tragedy. I seem to remember the headlines. Something to do with a rail accident just outside of Paddington Station."

The need to curl into the fetal position tried to take control of her. She fought it.

He nodded, as though he suddenly remembered. "My mother," he said with a curiously gentle smile, "thinks you are the finest actress of your generation. She wept as she told me. You lost your husband and your children. Two boys."

"Good God!" Baldy exploded beside her. "Why not just smash her in the face with your Uzi?" He leaned toward her protectively. "You might be able to explain away murder as serving your cause, but torture only proves you a villain."

The man didn't even turn Baldy's way. His dark eyes, compassionate under their fervor, held hers.

"I mean you no pain, *madame.* I have lost friends and family in this campaign and I mention it only to remind you that life *must* go on. If we lose heart, we lose everything."

"Mine was ripped out," she replied. "I no longer have one."

He put a hand to her knee and patted gently, the gesture curiously fraternal. "Ah, but you do. It sleeps after great tragedy, but it will stir again. There is still passion in you onstage."

She shrugged. "When I'm onstage, that isn't me. I'm someone else. And there's no one to pay my ransom. I have no family left. I'm afraid I'll have to be a political statement rather than a continuation of your work."

He frowned at her. "It alarms me that you would prefer that. I see it in your eyes." Then he smiled. "I know you have a father who loves you very much."

She sat up in alarm. "It would be cruel to frighten an old man for nothing. I assure you he has no money to pay a ransom for me."

One of his men shouted to him and beckoned him with the radio. He rose gracefully to his feet and shook his head at her. "Take a breath, *madame*. Inhale the wind and the night. There is much to live for."

"Do *not* call my father," she ordered his retreating figure.

He didn't hear her. Or if he did, his cause was more important than her concerns for a lonely old man.

"It'll be okay, love," Baldy comforted, nudging her with his shoulder. "There'll be a public outcry when the world learns we've been taken. The army will mobilize. Citizens will arm themselves with torches and pitchforks and come to our aid."

"You're the one lost in a script, Baldy," she said grimly, stretching gingerly to try to ease the pain in her shoulders. She longed for the moment a little while ago when she hadn't really cared whether she lived or died.

Now she was worried about her father.

Chapter One

June 23, 7:05 p.m.
Lamplight Harbor, Maine

Duffy March was already formulating a plan as he listened to Elliott Lawton wind up the story of his daughter's kidnapping. Under the professional assessment of danger, and the knowledge that he'd have to argue for a place among the gendarmes responding to the scene, was the awareness that this was the scenario he used to dream about when he was eight and Maggie was his sixteen-year-old babysitter. Her father worked for the State Department, while his taught history at Georgetown University.

Then nothing had separated them but eight years and a stockade fence between his parents' property in Arlington and the Lawtons', but that had changed considerably since she'd moved to Europe.

She was now the much-adored star of the London stage, and the widow of a prominent banker, while he was the single father of two, who owned and operated a security company. He had a staff of forty who'd helped him acquire a worldwide reputation among the noble and the famous who needed protection. The living was good, with a penthouse apartment in Manhattan and a very large waterfront home on the coast of Maine where he and the boys spent the summers.

"What I fear the most," Elliott confided as he paced the broad deck that looked out on the ocean, "is that…she'll be happy to let it all go bad."

Charlie March, Duffy's father, who'd flown the light plane that had brought them here from Arlington right after the State Department called Charlie with the news, caught his friend's arm and pushed him into a chair. "Sit down, Elliott, before we have to resuscitate you."

Charlie sat beside him and shook his head grimly at his son. "She's had a sort of death wish since she lost Harry and the boys. He's afraid she'll do something reckless and…you know."

"Tell me you can go to France," Elliott pleaded, on his feet and ignoring his drink. "I know the gendarmes will do all they can, but with six hostages and men with guns everywhere, I'm so afraid she'll literally get caught in the crossfire. I can get you clearance to accompany them. And you have your own connections there, don't you? Didn't you work for a member of the French parliament once?"

He nodded. Gaston Dulude, who'd waged war against a band of French drug dealers, had wanted protection for his wife and himself as the case went to trial.

"Of course I'll go to France," Duffy assured him, "but my housekeeper's on vacation. You'll have to stay with Mike and Adam, Dad."

Charlie nodded. "Of course."

"I'll stay, too," Elliott promised. "What can we do to help you get ready?"

"You can get me that clearance, Mr. Lawton," Duffy said, pointing to the phone, "while I get myself a flight to Paris."

"Just get packed," Elliott said. "I'll get you a plane, too."

As Duffy headed for the stairs, the back door slammed and his boys came racing through the kitchen into the living room. They'd been at a birthday party for the Baker twins, boys Mike's age who lived two doors over.

Mike, seven, led the way, stick-straight black hair flopping in his eyes, the red sweater and jeans that had been pristine just a few hours ago now smeared with food or finger paints, or both. Four-year-old Adam followed in his dust, the food and finger paints smeared across his face as well as his clothes. He had Lisa's fair good looks and passionate personality.

The boys ignored Duffy completely and went straight for their grandfather. "I saw your car, Grandpa!" Mike exclaimed.

Wisely, Charlie sat down as Mike flew into his lap. Adam followed, wrapping his arm gleefully around his grandfather's neck. Duffy saw Elliott turn away, holding the phone to his ear and blocking the other so that he could hear, using the call as an excuse to be able to focus his attention elsewhere.

It had to be hard for him, Duffy guessed, to see Charlie enveloped by his grandchildren when he'd never see his own again.

"Are you staying for dinner?" Mike asked.

As Duffy topped the stairs, he heard his father reply that he was staying a little longer than that.

Duffy had packed a small bag, made a call to his office in New York and was ready to go when the boys rushed into his room as though pursued. Mike always traveled at top speed, and Adam was determined that his older brother never escape him.

Duffy sat on the edge of his bed to explain his sudden departure.

"When are you coming back?" Mike climbed up next to him and leaned into his arm, looking worried. "Grandpa said he didn't know."

"I think three or four days," Duffy replied, lifting Adam onto his knee. "If it's going to be longer, I'll call you."

"Grandpa said you're going to help a friend."

"Yes."

"He said bad guys took her and you have to get her back."

"Yes. But I'm going to have a lot of help."

Mike sighed. "You won't get shot, right, 'cause you always know what you're doing?"

Duffy liked to think Mike's faith in him wasn't

misplaced. "That's right. I'll be fine. And so will she. I'll be back home before you know it."

"You're friends with a *girl?*" Adam asked. He screwed up his pink-cheeked face into a ripple of nose, lips and chin, and crossed his bright blue eyes. "We don't have any girls around here 'cause we don't like 'em."

Duffy laughed and squeezed him close. "I like them. I just don't happen to have one. But I would if I could."

That was apparently beyond Adam's comprehension. "They're silly and they're afraid of snakes."

"I thought you were afraid of snakes," Mike needled.

Adam shrugged off the reminder. "That was when I was little."

Mike rolled his eyes at Duffy. "He's a real giant now," he said under his breath.

Adam socked him on the shoulder.

Duffy caught his hand and reminded, "Hey! No hitting, remember? And no giving Grandpa any trouble while I'm gone. He's getting older and he can't chase you down or climb trees to get you when you've gone too high."

"If we're perfect," Mike bargained, "can we go to Disney World before summer's over?"

They'd talked about that a few times during the year, and though Duffy had made no promises, it was on his agenda.

"You think you can be perfect?" Duffy teased Mike.

Mike nodded, then qualified that with his head

tilted in Adam's direction. "But I'm not sure he can do it."

"I can, too!" Adam raised a fist to punch him again, then at Duffy's expression, thought better of it and withdrew it. "What is perfect?"

"It means really, really good," Mike informed him. "No mistakes."

Duffy lifted Adam onto his hip and let Mike drag his overnight bag toward the stairs. "Perfect's a little hard to strive for. Just listen to Grandpa, stay in the yard like you're supposed to, unless Grandpa says it's okay to go next door, and eat your vegetables."

Adam made another face as they started down the stairs. "What if Grandpa makes eggplant like Desiree does sometimes?"

"I'll ask him not to." Duffy turned to Mike, who struggled with the bag. "Want me to take that?"

Mike shook his head. "I got it, Dad."

Duffy watched Mike with love and pride, and thought as he had many times over the past three years, that taking him had been one of the best moves he'd ever made.

At the bottom of the stairs, Charlie took the bag from Mike.

"I'm flying you to Kennedy," he said, "to meet an old CIA pal of Elliott's who's taking you to Paris. Elliott's staying with the boys."

"Tell him about the eggplant!" Adam whispered loudly in Duffy's ear.

THE FOLLOWING DAY Duffy lay on his stomach in the grass at the top of a slope in the Pyrenees. A dozen gendarmes were ranged around him, looking down on the Basque camp in the meadow below. The air was sweet with wildflowers, the whispered sounds around him spoken in an unfamiliar language, and somewhere in that meadow, the woman who'd saved his life when she was a teenager waited for rescue. It if weren't for the glare in his eyes and the itch of grass and insects under his black sweater, he'd think this wasn't real.

But it was. He peered through binoculars to the scene below and saw men in camouflage and berets—the separatists. Then he noticed two men, hands tied behind their backs, sitting under a tree, and two women, hands also tied, one lying on the ground, presumably asleep, the other walking agitatedly back and forth. She was slender and moved as though she was young. He tried to focus on their faces, but they were too far away.

Maggie was blond, though, and both women were dark-haired. He scanned the camp for some sign of her and the third man. He finally spotted them across the camp, sitting back to back. It looked as though they were talking.

He focused on the woman as closely as he could and saw long, disheveled hair the color of polished gold. The sun picked it out like a mirror and made a halo around it. He couldn't see her face, just a pair of long legs bent at the knee in camel-colored pants.

He turned the glasses to the man she leaned against and saw that he was about her height, in a baseball cap and glasses also picked out by the sun. They were exhausted, judging by the way they leaned on each other.

It had been almost twenty hours since they'd been taken, and he could only imagine their weariness and fear. It was clearly visible in the woman pacing back and forth.

Instinct demanded that he run down the slope now, a full clip in his Glock. Reason, fortunately, dictated otherwise. Count men and weapons. Memorize positions. Rest and wait for darkness.

That was exactly the order passed on to him in broken English from the young captain lying prone beside him.

His eyes burned with the strain of keeping track of that spot of gold in the distance. Just as dusk turned to darkness, he watched one of the men in camouflage hook an arm into Maggie's and help her to her feet. Then he did the same for the man. He led them to the fire and ladled them bowls of food.

Then it became too dark to see details. The campfire flickered in the blackness, and finally the moon appeared from behind a cloud to cast a frail light on the camp. He searched it for a glimpse of gold and spotted it near the tree where the two men had sat. He thought he saw the agitated young woman near her, but he couldn't be sure.

The air crackled with tension as the order came to move down the slope. Duffy, focused on that glimpse of gold, stayed on the flank so that he could move out in an instant.

"I CAN NOT STAND IT another moment!" Celine whispered in heavily accented English. Her mouth trembled and her whole body shook. She'd been on the brink of hysteria since they'd been ambushed on the hiking trail in the park, and was now about to plunge over the edge.

"It's going to be all right," Maggie told her as she'd done a dozen times since this nightmare had begun.

But as the girl continued to whine, Maggie was distracted by something she couldn't quite define, some subtle disturbance of air she felt rather than heard. She turned toward the rugged slope just beyond their camp, wondering if she was imagining things.

There was nothing to see in the pale moonlight, but she noticed that the leader, Eduard, had sensed something, too. His men seemed unaware of anything, but Baldy came up beside her. With the actor's gift for feeling what couldn't be seen, he asked under his breath, "What is it?"

Before she could answer, Eduard shouted something to his men as he shrugged the Uzi off his shoulder and aimed it toward the slope. Two of their captors came running toward the hostages and tried to round them up and lead them into the trees.

But Celine screamed, now clearly in a panic, and ran in the other direction.

One of the soldiers aimed his weapon at her and shouted something that was probably a command to stop.

Maggie, already in pursuit of her, doubted that she heard the order.

"Celine!" she shouted. "Get down!"

But Celine hadn't heard her, either.

The order was issued again and punctuated with the sound of gunfire.

Maggie ran faster, so close to Celine that she could have touched her had her hands not been tied. Her only hope was to throw herself at the girl and knock her to the ground before a bullet did.

But before she could do that, something struck her from the side and knocked her off her feet. For a surprised instant she simply lay in the cool grass hearing the sounds of chaos in the camp. There were cries, gunfire, shouted commands. She heard Celine's sobbing.

Then she became aware of the weight stifling her and struck backward with an elbow, certain the Basque gunman had caught them.

"Whoa! I...oof!" She flailed and kicked like a wild thing, the part of her mind not occupied with the struggle wondering why she was doing it when she didn't care if she lived or died. Then she decided it was probably a matter of being able to decide for herself when and where she gave up.

Her foot had connected with flesh, and she took advantage of her opponent's momentary surprise to scramble to her feet and run in the direction of Celine's sobs.

But she didn't get far. She was tackled around the

ankles and went down with a thud. She turned with a scream of rage, flailing wildly in the dark, trying to sit up.

"Maggie!"

A flash exploded just as a hand shoved her back to the grass, and there was a grunt of pain as her attacker went down. Then another flash lit the night right beside her, and a man in camouflage fell across her body.

Even as the horror of the moment chilled her through, her brain was working on what was out of place here.

Then she realized what it was. The man she'd tried to fight off had called her Maggie in perfect, unaccented English. She also realized that the shot intended for her had caught him. God. Had she gotten one of their rescuers killed?

No. An instant later the body of the man who'd fallen across her was dragged off and she was turned onto her face as more gunfire rattled overhead. The man's weight held her down, and she heard the deafening sound of his weapon and the thump of another body not too far away.

Then everything grew quiet.

"Monsieur March?" a voice with a rolling French accent whispered in the stillness. "You are well?"

"We're fine," he replied. "You?"

"*Oui.* But you were hit, no?"

"Yes. It's just a scrape. Is the woman all right?"

"She has fainted."

The man holding Maggie down said wryly, "If only I'd been that lucky."

Maggie tried to turn, but the hand continued to hold her down. "Lie still," the man commanded, "until we get the all-clear."

"I'm sorry." Maggie spoke into the grass. "But when a man tackles a woman to the ground she presumes she's not going to like whatever he has planned."

"My plans were to prevent you from getting shot," he countered, then added on a note of amusement, "Unfortunately, you didn't have the same plans for me."

She sighed and dropped her forehead to the grass. "Again, I'm sorry. It was dark. You were running after me…"

"It's all right. I'm fine."

A shout came from the main part of the camp, and the man got to his feet, pulling her with him. "All clear, Maggie. Pretty soon you'll be home."

There was her name again, spoken in that familiar way. She stopped as he began to lead her to the main part of the camp, now well lit with flashlights and emergency flares. He had hold of her arm and stopped with her, a dark eyebrow raised in question.

She looked into dark-brown eyes, their expression curiously satisfied and relaxed considering what he'd just been through. His nose was strong and straight, his mouth half smiling, his chin a square line in an angular face. Short, dark-brown hair was ruffled by the night wind.

She shuddered as the cool air rippled through her light jacket. She had the oddest sense of familiarity without recognizing his features. "Do I know you?" she asked.

DUFFY COULDN'T BELIEVE how beautiful she still was. The teenager with whom he'd been infatuated was still visible in the smooth curve of her cheek, the youthful tilt of her nose, and the natural color of the long, straight hair he'd been able to pick out from a distance. But pain had worn away the sparkle he remembered in her dark-blue eyes. The ever-ready smile wasn't there, either.

Of course, she'd just been through a great trial, but he had a feeling that wasn't the problem. There was a certain flatness in her glance that had probably been there for a while, a disturbingly even rhythm to her speech and movements that seemed to indicate a lack of interest. Though, when she'd thought he represented death just a few moments ago, she'd fought him like a tiger. He wondered if the lack of interest was something she'd simply decided upon rather than something she sincerely felt.

He ripped off the black sweater he wore and pushed it on over her head, pulling it down over her thin jacket.

She looked surprised and seemed about to protest when the warmth of it apparently penetrated and she rubbed her arms to help it along.

"You once knew me very well," he replied, drawing her with him toward the group. Eduard's men had been handcuffed and were already being sent down the mountain with the Gendarmes. "You stayed the night with me many times."

Now she raised an eyebrow. "I did?"

"You did. We sat up until all hours talking."

She was staring at him in complete confusion, her pale lips temptingly parted. He had to look away from them.

"You made caramel corn and brownies," he went on, "and we watched *Dallas* together."

He saw realization light up her eyes. Then she gasped and pushed him with both hands. "Duffy March!" she exclaimed, smiling, and shoved him again. Then she wrapped her arms around him and held him tightly.

Her embrace was intense. He was smart enough to know it had nothing to do with him but with the fact that he was a tie to the happy life she'd lived before fame and tragedy had taken so much from her.

"Oh, Duffy," she whispered, clutching him even tighter.

He winced, a burning pinch on the outside of his upper arm.

"You've been shot!" she exclaimed, ripping a scarf from around her neck and holding it to his blood-soaked sleeve.

"Just nicked me," he said, drawing her back into his arms.

He kissed the top of her head and held her close. "Hi, Maggie," he said.

Chapter Two

"But what are you *doing* here?" she demanded, still smiling.

"Your father sent me," he replied. She'd stopped in her tracks again and he coaxed her forward. "It's kind of a long story and should probably be saved for the ride home. Right now the police will want to talk to you."

It was several hours before the police were finished with Maggie and her party, and a doctor took care of Duffy's shoulder. Duffy called home to tell her father that she was safe.

"Thank God!" he exclaimed prayerfully, then added, "I owe you, son."

"I was happy to help."

"Will you ask her to call me when you finally get her home? It doesn't matter what time."

"She's insisting on flying home tonight, so it'll probably be early morning."

"I'll wait for your call."

Her friends were all going back to the count's

place to recover from the ordeal, but Maggie declined his invitation.

"You're going to fly to London tonight?" the man she'd introduced as her agent asked. "That'll be exhausting."

"I'm already exhausted," she replied, giving him a hug. "And my friend, here, has gotten us a flight." Then she hugged the rest of the group in turn.

He blessed her father's CIA connections as he happily accepted her praise and gratitude.

They caught up on the way home—what she'd been doing, what he'd been doing.

She skipped over the loss of her husband and children with a falsely philosophical "And every life has its ups and downs, my downs were just more abysmal than most people's." Then she gave him a phony smile. "But my career's ongoing, I work all the time, and I like that. When did you go into security?"

"After the Army. I was young and strong and felt invincible." He reached overhead to adjust the air in her direction. "I guess there just wasn't enough threat to my life, so I went looking for it in other people's by going to work as a bodyguard. Went off on my own after a year. Our headquarters are in New York, but we work all over the world."

"I love New York. It's like a slightly less dignified London."

They compared lives in the big city, she told him she did needlework for relaxation and he told her he loved to prowl garage sales, refinish old furniture, make useful items out of junk and that one day when he retired he would open a shop.

"I'm never going to retire," she said in the taxi that drove them from Heathrow to Wandsworth Common, a tony part of London. "They're going to have to drag me off the stage when I die in Baldy's arms."

"Baldy?"

"My actor friend. You met him at the police station. The one with the attitude. We work together a lot."

"Isn't his wife jealous?" He couldn't imagine any woman willingly letting her husband kiss Maggie Lawton, whether it was in the script or not.

She shook her head. "After three wives, he's a confirmed bachelor. And since all his wives were actresses, the fact that I'm a confirmed bachelor girl simplifies his life. Saves him from falling in love with me." She added as an aside, "He always falls in love with his leading lady."

"Isn't it bad for an actor to be so confused?"

"Not at all. Being unable to tell your real life from your stage life is the sign of a good actor."

"How do you stay sane that way?"

She rolled her head on the back of the cab's upholstery and grinned at him. "Who told you actors were sane?"

Her home was unlike anything he'd ever seen, except in movies. The substantial Victorian she lived in was huge and almost two hundred years old, similar in design to the other residences near the lush park.

The grass, the potted flowers in the doorway and the rich vanilla color of the stone walls glistened in the early morning light as she unlocked her door.

Inside, the ceilings were high, the windows long and draped in gold brocade. Off-white silk fabric adorned the walls, which were hung with paintings that he guessed were originals.

The furnishings were formal and elegant, he noted, as he wandered after Maggie through a vast living room with a marble fireplace and up a mahogany staircase to an upstairs flooded with sunlight.

"Eponine is away for a week, thank God," she said as she pushed open a door and gestured him inside. "Or she'd be weeping all over me. She's very emotional."

"Friend? Housekeeper?"

"Both," she replied. "I've tried to talk her into auditioning for a role. I think she'd be a natural. But she says she'd worry about who would take care of me."

He had to meet this Eponine, he thought. And put her mind to rest.

"I promised your father you'd call him as soon as you got home," he said as he walked into a bedroom decorated in brown and gold, with old maps on the wall and a fireplace. Everything required for a small office was at one end, while the other was set up for luxurious sleeping. He whistled softly at the elegance of it.

He wondered if this had been her husband's office but didn't want to ask.

"I sold the house in Devon when…after the accident." She hesitated only an instant, but the quick diversion suggested she still couldn't say, "when they died." He could certainly understand that. He couldn't imagine losing his boys and ever coming to a point when he could accept it.

"I've always loved the city," she went on, going to a door at the far end of the room to show him there was a very elegant bathroom there complete with hot tub. "You can't be lonely here. There's always someplace to go and something to do."

He wasn't sure why, but the words didn't ring true. He was sure there was always someplace to go and something to do, but he didn't think that assuaged her loneliness.

"Have a hot bath and a good sleep," she said, blowing him a kiss, "and I'll take you somewhere wonderful for dinner. Then we can arrange to send you home on the Concorde."

She closed the door on him before he could tell her that he might go home on the Concorde, but he wasn't going alone.

MAGGIE DIDN'T KNOW why she was shaking. She didn't think this was fear. She'd kept her head throughout their captivity—well, except for when she'd mistaken Duffy for one of her captors and that had been an honest mistake—and the danger was over now. Everything that could hurt her had been dealt with effectively by Duffy March and the gendarmerie.

So, why was she shaking? She'd showered, put on her favorite white silk negligee, then found herself trembling like a pudding. She had to pull Duffy's sweater back over her head to try to stop it.

Delayed reaction? she wondered, as she climbed in under the covers. But how could that be when she hadn't really cared what had happened? When she'd simply shut down everything that could make her care?

Then it came to her. It was Duffy. It was that glimpse of life as it had been once, when it all still lay ahead of her full of hope and expectation. It was remembering the heroic little boy he'd been, determined to battle the asthma that plagued him, so that he could live a normal life.

Well, he'd certainly done it, she thought, reaching for her address book and phone. He'd grown tall and strong with the proportions and confidence of a tested athlete. She guessed he'd outgrown the asthma. She remembered that he'd embarked on a regimen to strengthen his muscles—and had been smart enough to know that the plan should include his brain. They'd often done homework together when she'd stayed with him, she fighting to understand the secrets of geometry that eluded her, and he doing extra reading in the subjects that interested him.

She closed her eyes and thought, with a lessening of the tremors, that it was good she'd had that glimpse of the old days. She could never be that Maggie again, but it was good to remember—though not for too long.

It wasn't going to help to call her father, but she had to. She knew how much he worried about her in normal circumstances; she could just imagine what her kidnapping had done to him. She hadn't seen him since the funeral, had resisted his pleas that she come home for a visit, because she'd have to be herself at home and she couldn't face that yet. She got by only by playing role after role that allowed her to be someone else.

"Oh, Maggie!" he breathed when he heard her voice. "Sweetheart, I was so worried about you."

"I know, Dad. I'm sorry." She was grateful that her voice sounded strong and even. "I'm fine, I promise. And it's such a treat to see Duffy."

"I knew he'd keep you safe."

"That he did."

"Maggie…" He paused and she knew he was building up to something. "I want you to come home for a visit."

"Daddy, I want to," she lied, "but I have eight performances a week and I…"

"Don't you have an understudy or something? I mean, didn't someone else have to go on for you while you were kidnapped?"

She searched her mind frantically for a viable excuse.

"And, you know, I don't like to worry *you,* but I haven't been all that well since the attack, and I'd like to know…"

She sat up and leaned forward. "What attack?"

He hesitated.

''What attack?'' she repeated.

''The heart attack.''

Her first thought was that he was putting her on—manipulating her. But he'd never done that before. And since she'd lost Harry and the boys, he tried particularly hard not to worry her.

''When did this happen?'' she demanded. ''Why didn't you tell me?''

''Well…because I was only in the hospital a few days, and the doctor said it was just a sort of warning to be careful. So I've been careful.''

He'd been careful, but her kidnapping probably hadn't done much to keep him calm.

''Okay, Dad,'' she said. ''I'll come. But I have to work it out with my director.''

''I'd love that, Maggie.'' He sounded relieved.

She promised to do it soon and let him know her plans. Then she hung up the phone and lay stiffly against the headboard, feeling those curious tremors coming on again.

She couldn't go home—but it sounded as though she had to. God.

She tried to make plans—to organize things in the hope it would make the tremors go away.

In the morning she'd call her travel agent to see about getting Duffy the next flight home on the Concorde. Then she'd call the bank and see about replacing her credit cards, her driver's license, all the things she'd lost when the kidnappers had taken her backpack from her. They were probably still somewhere on the mountain. Life was going to be very inconvenient until everything was replaced.

Then she'd call her director and see about getting a week off in July. Exhaustion overtook her despite the tremors, and she fell asleep, thinking that if she was going to go home, she'd have to do it as a star— not as the real Maggie Lawton. That was the only way she could protect herself.

SHE DREAMED OF EVERYTHING that had happened— of her and Baldy and the Thickes visiting Gerard to help celebrate his birthday. Of the argument over what to do with the Sunday afternoon, then the decision to go hiking in the park. She saw the remote uphill spot, heard Prissie's whiny remark about the trail being too steep and rocky, then the sudden appearance of men with Uzis.

She remembered very clearly the terror she'd felt that first instant. The absolutely horrifying threat she'd felt to her life and her safety. It had taken her a moment to remember that she didn't care whether she lived or died.

The dream proceeded just as events had happened, except that there was no rescue. The government refused to negotiate, her father never called for the now big and capable Duffy March to rescue his little girl, and the gentle and enigmatic Eduard aimed his Uzi at her and fired.

She awoke feeling the pain in her chest, gasping for air in a complete panic—the last two years of horror distilled into that one moment.

Her bedroom door burst open, and she saw Duffy hesitate in the doorway.

She said his name and reached a hand toward him, caught in a nebulous world somewhere between her dream and reality.

"What?" he asked, hurrying toward her. He sat on the bed beside her and wrapped an arm around her. "Nightmare?"

She put a hand to her stomach and held it up to show him the blood. "I've been shot!" she whispered. "You were...too late."

He put a hand to where her other hand pressed against her middle to stanch the flow of blood.

Damn the shaking! But she supposed if she was about to expire from a chest wound, she had the right to tremble.

"Maggie," he said, holding her hand up in front of her face. "You've been dreaming. No blood, see? You haven't been shot. You're fine."

"I am not fine!" she screamed at him. "I have a hole in my chest! Right...here!" She put a hand to the terrible burning pain and realized with the sudden clarity of wakefulness that it was an old pain. It wasn't from a bullet at all, but from a two-year-old grief she was not going to be able to survive.

And now that she'd acknowledged it, the pain became more than she could bear. It had barbs and tentacles she'd controlled by suppressing it, but they now beat her and choked her and made her cry out in anguish.

She heard herself sob.

She fought to escape, but the pain was tenacious and no matter how hard she struggled, she couldn't get free.

DUFFY DIDN'T KNOW what to do but hold her. At first she fought him, screaming, then she clung to him and sobbed. She was wearing his sweater, and she felt slight and fragile under its folds. He wrapped his arms tightly around her as she trembled and wept, concluding that the nightmare must have triggered a response to her ordeal that somehow related to the pain of the past two years of her life.

"It's okay, Maggie," he whispered, rocking her in the middle of the bed. "You're going to survive."

"I don't think so," she replied, finally quieting.

"You will," he insisted firmly.

She stopped crying and leaned against him, tired and dispirited. "Most of the time I don't even want to," she said.

"You have to," he said firmly. "You still have a father, you still have friends and, from what I read, you still have quite an audience."

She leaned slightly away from him to look into his eyes. Hers were still filled with tears. His heart bled for her.

"You didn't tell me my father had had a heart attack," she said, her tone mildly accusing. "I'm surprised your father didn't write or call me."

For a minute he didn't know what to say. He saw a pitcher of water and a cup on her beside table and reached for it to cover up his confusion. As far as he knew, Elliott hadn't had a heart attack. He didn't know everything that went on in the Lawtons' lives, but his father usually kept him up on the important things. He couldn't imagine he would have let that slip by.

"Where'd you hear that?" he asked, pouring water into the cup and handing it to her.

"Thank you. From my father! He told me when he was trying to get me to come home." She looked at him with sudden suspicion as she sipped from the cup. "Or, didn't it happen? I didn't want to go home and he might have been …"

"Ah…well, I'm not sure. My father's always trying to protect me, too. I know he's been worried about your dad, so it's entirely possible." That was partly true. His father was always worried about his friend, who, at sixty-four, took off on nebulous missions for the State Department as though he was still a man in his prime. He just wasn't sure he was worried about Elliott's heart.

Duffy was suddenly distracted from that puzzle when he became aware of a subtle tension in the air. The intimacy of their embrace in the middle of the bed, hardly necessary now that she was composed again seemed to be generating it.

He knew she was aware of it, too, when her eyes met his in confused surprise. Using her hands on the mattress for leverage, she pushed herself slightly away from him. He noticed for the first time the tailored white silk nightshirt she wore—and the length of slender leg it revealed.

"I…I'm going to try to get time off," she said a little distractedly, "sometime in July."

He stood, going to the window and pushing her draperies back. The sun was low, long shadows falling across the park. The beautiful setting made him inexplicably homesick.

"Why don't you just come home with me?" he suggested.

She blinked, surprised by the suggestion. "I can't do that," she said.

"Why not?"

"Because I'm the lead in a play," she replied, her eyes a little desperate. "Because all my credit cards are in a gully somewhere in the Pyrenees. Because…"

"I can't imagine your boss refusing you a couple of weeks R and R after what you've been through. And I'll spring for your airfare and lend you some money until you get the credit cards straightened out."

"I can't leave the country without my passport." She looked satisfied with that excuse. Even proud of it. "I've misplaced it in the shuffle of bags and reporters and hurry."

He spotted her things apparently thrown carelessly on a chair when she'd changed for bed last night and saw her passport pinned to her bra strap. He hooked the lacy lavender thing in one finger and held it up, the book dangling.

"I'll make reservations for two, then," he said.

"Give your father some peace of mind and you a probably much-needed rest."

That surprised look she'd given him a moment ago registered a little longer, then turned to annoyance. She pushed herself to her feet with a sudden, imperious expression, intended, he was sure, to put him in his place.

"Look, Duffy," she said, tossing her hair. He guessed she probably did that onstage. It was very effective. "I'm so grateful you came all this way to see to my safety. But that's accomplished. I'm free now and our long friendship notwithstanding, your services are terminated."

"Now, don't get in a huff because I caught you in a fib," he said. "I understand why you don't want to go home, but that isn't healthy. And if you're going to get on with your life, you have to get serious about dealing with reality."

"What do you know about dealing with reality?" she demanded, anger igniting in her eyes. "You own a penthouse apartment in Manhattan, and your business has offices in five countries. Your failures and your grief are still ahead of you."

He arched an eyebrow at the deliberate ploy to gain the upper hand.

"Not so," he corrected amiably. "I know about loss, if not death, and, being a bodyguard, I know that hiding doesn't defeat your enemy. It just holds him off until the next time he finds you." Then he smiled. "And while you might have been able to order me around when I was eight, things have changed considerably. Part of the deal when your father hired me was that I take you home. So the job isn't done until I deliver you to Arlington.''

''I'm not ready to go yet.''

He spread both arms in a gesture of patience. ''Then do what has to be done and I'll wait.''

The room suddenly exploded in heavy perfume and rolling *R*s when a very short, very hefty woman hurried in, moving a little like a tank in a blue dress with white polka dots and white tennis shoes. Her permed hair was a brassy shade of red.

''Madame Lawton!'' the woman exclaimed. She'd apparently been crying and continued to sob as she rolled into the room and wrapped a very surprised Maggie in her embrace.

Maggie disappeared for a moment, and all Duffy heard was a thin, high-pitched, ''Eponine! I thought you were on vacation!''

''*Mais oui,* but I heard the news!'' Eponine said, taking a tissue from her pocket and dabbing her eyes with it. ''I knew you would need me! Are you all right? Did they savage you?''

''Of course not,'' Maggie replied. ''I'm perfectly all right. There was no reason for you to spoil your trip.''

''Oh, but I could not leave you alo—'' She stopped abruptly when she noticed Duffy standing bare-chested at the foot of the bed. She looked confused at first, then, after a head-to-toe scan, apparently decided the situation was not all that complicated.

''Oh, *monsieur,* I'm so sorry. *Madame,* please forgive me." She put her fingertips to her mouth and turned in an embarrassed circle.

"No, no, no!" Maggie emphatically denied the woman's assumption. Eponine took a step back in surprise at her vehemence. Duffy stood his ground. "It isn't that at all. This is an old friend of mine from home," she said with a glance at Duffy that suggested the term *friend* hung in the balance.

Eponine gave Duffy a sidelong glance that spoke volumes. "Friends are the most dangerous threat to a woman's peace of mind because they become lovers so easily."

Maggie shook her head. "He's almost ten years younger than I am."

Eponine drew a dreamy breath. "Ah, *madame*. That is even more *merveilleux*."

"It's eight years," Duffy corrected, "and I'll wager I'm far more experienced. You settled down with a family while I've never been married."

Annoyed that she was losing control of the situation, Maggie said irritably, "Well, what does that have to do with anything?"

"I didn't think it had anything to do with it," Duffy replied, "but it seemed important to you."

"Are you hungry?" she asked in that same impatient tone.

"Yes."

"Eponine, you may stay to fix dinner for which I'll add an extra day on to your vacation, then you must get back to your daughter."

Eponine winked at Duffy. *"Oui, madame."*

WHILE EPONINE PUTTERED in the kitchen and Duffy went off to make phone calls, Maggie took another shower, desperate to clear her addled brain.

Her life was growing more out of control by the moment. For years she'd been experiencing this hole in the center of her world that refused to heal, then she was kidnapped like some cabin boy in a novel, held at gunpoint, rescued by the boy she used to baby-sit more than twenty years ago, and now her maid thought they were having an affair. Her and Duffy March!

And he was turning out to be a surprise. The sweet, cooperative, well-behaved little boy who'd hung on her every word was now a stubborn, autocratic, know-it-all, who seemed to forget she had a mind of her own.

She was drying her hair when there was a loud rap on her half-open bathroom door. Duffy peered around it and handed her the phone. "Picked up this call for you. David Styron?"

She gave him a cool glance and took the phone. "Thank you. David?"

"Yes, Mags." The large voice that could be heard from the back of the balcony boomed over the phone. Maggie had to hold it slightly away from her ear. "Glen tells me that you and Baldy are both well, but in need of a break after your ordeal. The devil's negotiated you a month's break—with pay—starting today."

"What?" She turned to Duffy, suspecting his hand in this, but he was gone.

"What?"

"That's right, my love. A whole month off. You must go to Cap Ferrat or someplace equally decadent and do nothing. But don't get too tanned now, will you, or Nancy will have trouble making you up."

"But, David, a month seems—"

"Long, yes I know. But Glen was insistent. He and Prissie are going to Bimini. And you mustn't worry, Sukie Darwin was really quite good as Lady Bellows last night. She's learned a lot watching you."

Maggie didn't know whether to be happy or upset. The fact that one's understudy had been "really quite good" was good and bad news. She was very much aware that the theater was filled with younger and probably more talented women who could replace her in a moment. But it was startling to hear it confirmed.

"Don't worry about a thing," David insisted. "Just rest and recover, and come back to us in time for the London Women's Charity night at the end of July. They've bought out the house and they'll want to see *you*."

Okay, that restored a modicum of her confidence.

"Thank you, David."

"Take care, Mags."

Damn. Now she had to go home. She closed her eyes against images of the three-story house, narrow and tall and happily ensconced in its downtown environment right next door to the Marches' place.

Her mother had always been home, but Duffy's mother had been a lawyer in her husband's firm, and they'd been gone a lot of the time. The bank account Maggie had built up watching Duffy for them had paid all her incidental expenses her first year of college.

Then she'd been discovered by a film agent in her second year. He'd come to watch his daughter perform in *The Rainmaker* and had been impressed with Maggie's portrayal of Lizzie. He'd offered to represent her, found her a bit part in a small film that was being shot in London.

There she'd met Harry Paget, a banker, and when the film wrapped, she'd stayed to marry him and trade the screen for the stage. She'd never regretted it.

Morgan and Alan had been born eleven months apart when she was in her middle twenties. When they were babies, they'd traveled with her everywhere, and when they were old enough to go to school, the theater had allowed her to spend afternoons with them before her performances.

Life had been good. The boys had been tall and blond like their father, with his tendency to take themselves seriously yet laugh at everything else. She'd found her husband and her boys endlessly fascinating.

Her parents had loved them, too, and when her mother died five years ago, her father had stayed with them for a month, trying to figure out how to go on.

Now that she'd experienced the same loss, she couldn't imagine how he'd managed.

She looked at herself in the mirror and saw Lady Bellows, the role she'd played for the past eighteen months. She wore designer suits, though at the moment it was a pale-orange peignoir set, wore her hair in a chignon and held her chin in the air. Her staff adored her, but her butler feared her sexual appeal.

Good. She would hide in character as long as she was able.

She walked into the kitchen to find Duffy and Eponine sharing a bottle of wine and a plate of broiled shrimp. They were laughing together, and she was surprised to feel a twinge of jealousy. Not for the alliance they seemed to have formed, she told herself, but for the laughter.

"Seems I've been given a month's leave from the play," she said, taking a chair opposite Duffy and smiling blandly at him as she reached for a shrimp. Eponine poured wine into the empty glass at her place. "You wouldn't know anything about that?"

He met her gaze with innocence in his. "Now, how could I have accomplished that while drinking wine with Eponine?"

"I don't know," she replied, then nipped the shrimp in two.

"Though you did manage to find me in a remote spot in the Pyrenees. You appear to be a resourceful man."

"But I had the French army on my side then."

She glanced at her housekeeper, who also returned

her a look of suspicious innocence. ''Eponine has a lot in common with the French army.''

''So, this means we'll be flying back together?'' he asked.

She admitted defeat, if only to herself. She had to see her father, and putting it off until July would have served no purpose anyway.

''I'm not sure I'll be able to pay my way,'' she reminded him. ''I'll go to the bank in the morning, but with all my credit cards missing, and most of my assets in stocks and real estate, I may not be able to get much cash.''

''You can owe me,'' he said with a grin.

That was precisely what she didn't want to do.

Chapter Three

The flight to the States the following afternoon seemed interminable, and was made even longer by the knowledge that she had only seventeen dollars in a purse she hated. According to the bank manager she'd spoken to that morning, her accounts had been frozen because Eduard had escaped capture and had apparently used one of her credit cards somewhere in Spain. In an effort to track him down, they wanted to stop any other activity on her accounts. They regretted the inconvenience. Not enough, she was sure.

She'd spent the next two hours scouring clothing and old purses for money left in pockets or coin compartments. Then, to add insult to injury, she had to put what she found in a brown leather pouch purse she'd never liked because everything sank to the bottom in it. Someday she was going to pummel Eduard herself for tossing her favorite ergonomic bag into a crevasse.

"I can't believe it," she grumbled, not for the first time. "Twenty-two years an actress, high-yield stocks and bonds, carefully acquired real estate, and I have seventeen dollars to my name.''

That sounded like a pouty princess talking—or possibly, Lady Bellows. Good. She wasn't having to reach to stay in character.

Duffy wasn't sure what that was all about—residual stress from her ordeal, maybe. As a girl, she'd never been one to flaunt her beauty, her intelligence, her family's comfortable situation or her popularity. She'd been very real and able to lower herself to the level of a child who needed her friendship.

''I'll give you my American Express,'' he offered, ''if you're reluctant to take money from your father.''

She rolled her eyes. ''Why would I be more willing to take money from you than from him?''

''Because we broke the ice when I bought your ticket,'' he replied, knowing he was annoying her. He suspected that her life, her determination to live it onstage, was wobbling, and he was going to do all he could to topple it. ''It'll be easier the second time.'' He was going to give her a week with her father in Arlington, then he was going to invite them to Lamplight Harbor to visit. He wanted her to see where he lived, get to know his boys, relax.

Then he was going to do his damnedest to seduce her.

She closed her eyes against his candor and shook her head. ''I'm going to be happy to say goodbye to you when we reach Kennedy,'' she said. ''You were much sweeter as a boy than you are as a man.''

"A man has too much to do to be sweet," he countered. "And sweetness is generally not a favorable trait in a bodyguard, anyway."

She smiled reluctantly at that, then leaned back in her seat and studied him as though she was seeing the child and not the man. He didn't particularly like that. But having her attention in any way was a plus.

"You must have gotten over the asthma," she said. "All your efforts at bodybuilding certainly paid off."

He watched her eyes scan his shoulders, but inclined his head modestly and pretended not to notice. "Thank you. I stayed with it, then learned a lot in the Army. I did outgrow the asthma and am now disgustingly healthy."

"And a little overconfident."

"A bodyguard—like a cop—has to have presence. This time you wouldn't have to save me from the burning vaporizer. I could rescue you."

Her eyes widened and she turned toward him with a slight smile at that memory, forgetting that he annoyed her.

"I'd forgotten that!" she said, her eyes losing focus as she thought back.

He'd been eight years old and just getting over a cold, so his asthma had been very active. His parents were at a dinner meeting with a client, and his mother had placed a vaporizer at his bedside to ease his breathing.

Maggie had been in the kitchen downstairs, preparing dinner, when a short in the vaporizer had caused it to catch fire. It had ignited the decorative quilt that hung over his bed, and he'd barely found the air in his lungs to shout Maggie's name.

She'd appeared in an instant, hesitated only a second before unplugging the vaporizer, draping it with his blanket, and carrying the now smoking device into the bathroom where she dropped it in the tub and poured water on it. Then she ran back to yank the burning quilt off the wall and submerged it in the bathtub, too.

He always looked back on that as the moment he fell in love with her. She'd then put him in his parents' bed, brought him dinner, then cleaned up the mess while he ate.

"Of course, I killed the vaporizer, your blanket and that beautiful quilt," she remembered with a nostalgic smile.

"Maybe, but my father paid you with a hundred-dollar bill that night. You averted what might have been a real disaster."

She nodded, accepting praise with a light laugh. "If I hadn't saved you, you couldn't have grown up to be such a smart aleck."

"There, see. I knew it was all *your* fault."

The flight attendant arrived with a cell phone. "Miss Lawton?"

Maggie blinked in surprise. "Yes."

"The airport radioed the pilot with a call from your father. We have him on the pilot's cell phone."

She listened, looking surprised, then disappointed.

"What?" she exclaimed. "What about your heart?

What about...?'' She stopped abruptly, apparently forced to listen again.

"Dad, I'm sorry, too," she said finally, "but I'll be fine at the house. I don't want to...no, I know you worry, but you shouldn't. I'm fine. I can't impose on him like that."

She said placatingly, "Okay, fine. I'll put him on. But I'm telling you now, I'm staying in Arlington." She put her hand over the mouthpiece and fixed Duffy with a fierce expression. "My father's been called overseas—some problem setting up a new government—and he wants me to go home with you rather than stay alone in Arlington. I'm *not* doing that. You will tell him that you're very busy and you don't have time to entertain a houseguest. Have I made myself clear?"

"Very," he said amiably and took the phone she held out. "Hi, Elliott."

"Duff!" Elliott said, his voice urgent. "I'm so sorry to do this to you, but I've been called overseas. They're sending a chopper for me in twenty minutes. Would you mind very much taking Maggie home with you? I don't want her to be alone."

"I wouldn't mind at all," he replied.

Her expression darkened, though she obviously wasn't sure what he and her father were saying. She threatened him with a pointing finger to his chest. "No!" she whispered. "Say, no!"

"Yes, of course," he said into her glower. "I'll be happy to take her home with me. Don't worry.

Just do your job and know that she'll be safe and sound."

Maggie put both hands to her face and fell back into her chair.

Duffy hung up the phone and handed it back to the flight attendant with a smug "Thank you!"

"You'll like Lamplight Harbor." He held up Maggie's seat belt as the light went on.

"I'm going to Arlington," she said, lowering her hands to put her belt together with an angry snap.

"With what?" he asked. "I'm holding your ticket."

She threatened him with a look. "I'm going, anyway."

"How are you going to get there?"

"Rent a car." She wasn't seeing the problem.

"And what are you going to pay for it with?"

"With…" she began, then remembered that all she had was seventeen dollars and no credit cards. That wasn't going to get her a car.

She straightened in her seat and firmed her lips. She looked magnificent but not as confident as she probably imagined. "You're going to rent it for me. Or let me have my ticket."

He smiled. "Guess again, Lady Bellows." When she looked surprised that he knew the name of her current role, he explained, "Eponine told me you've played her for so many performances that you take on some of her qualities when you're stressed."

"Look," she said, clearly clutching her temper in

both hands, "I came to the States to see my father, not to visit Lightbulb…what is it?"

"Lamplight Harbor," he provided.

"Lamplight Harbor," she repeated, "so that you can get some kind of payback for all the years you had to do what I said, by bullying me. I'm forty years old, Duffy," she said with a sigh as though it were eighty. "And while some women love the forceful male, I've never been a fan. So, please. Lend me money to rent a car."

"I have no intention of bullying you," he said. "The deal I made with your father was to deliver you safely, and I…"

"I'm not a girl!" she said a little too loudly. Several nearby passengers turned to look at her. She lowered her voice. "I'm an adult woman," she said. "Almost middle-aged. No one has to deliver me from one man's hands to another's!"

He caught the hand with which she gestured emphatically. "You're thirty-nine," he corrected, "not forty. That's hardly middle-aged, and your father wants to know you're being looked after, not because he thinks you're not capable of caring for yourself, but because he loves you and you'll always be his little girl. So let a man with heart trouble have a little peace about the situation."

That last statement distracted her as he'd hoped it would. "He *does* have heart trouble?" she asked worriedly.

"I'm not sure," he replied, "but do we want to

risk worrying him further when he's in a tight spot as it is?''

She finally fell against her seat back with a groan. ''If you hadn't butted into my life,'' she said, ''I could be in my bathtub right now, listening to Russell Watson and planning to go to Le Caprice for dinner.''

''What were you going to buy dinner with?''

''Oh, shut up.''

HE CANCELED MAGGIE'S TICKET for the connecting flight to Virginia, then pushed the luggage cart toward the little blue American-made sedan rental at the end of an aisle. She carried his cappuccino and her caramel latte. He always preferred to drive home from New York, enjoying the beauty and peace and quiet. It gave him time to readjust from his work life to his life as a parent.

''I thought you intended to stay only for a week,'' he said, indicating her three large bags and train case. ''There must be enough clothes in there for a four-hour fashion show.''

''Ha, ha,'' she said, holding the cart handle while he unlocked the trunk. ''Nice clothes is one of the perks of being in the public eye. Designers court you.''

''Well, they'll certainly be able to find you. I'll probably have to rent a horse trailer to get it all home.''

''Or to hold all the horse stuff you're shoveling.''

He gave her a challenging look over his shoulder

as he rearranged her bags several times before making them fit. The cart empty, she handed him the drinks, then pushed it toward a cart rack at a midway point in the aisle and hurried back to the car.

In the front seat he placed their drinks in a caddy between the seats, then backed out of the lot and onto the road that would lead them to northbound traffic.

"How far?" she asked when they were firmly ensconced in rush hour traffic.

"A little over four hundred miles," he replied.

"So, we're not going to make it tonight."

"No. I thought we'd stay over in New Hampshire."

She didn't applaud the plan, but she didn't dispute it, either, so Duffy just drove. She fell asleep outside of Connecticut and he watched the traffic as he reached behind him for his jacket to drop it across her.

She looked troubled, even in sleep, he thought, and hoped he had what it took to pull her out of the past and into a future with him. He'd thought he would have to play it cool, give her time, invite her and her father to his home. But Elliott's sudden mission had been a fateful intervention forcing her into his path. He had to take advantage of it.

She awoke in northern Massachusetts. It was dusk.

She sat up guiltily and stretched, a gesture he was grateful he couldn't watch because of the thinning but steady traffic.

"Where are we?" she asked on a yawn.

"Almost to the New Hampshire border. You ready for dinner?"

"I'm starved," she admitted.

"Okay." He pointed to a highway sign that promised Good Food and Cozy Cabins. "Looks like a good place to spend the night."

The cabins were small and rustic, but each boasted a tidy bathroom and a television set. That was all Duffy needed, but after having seen Maggie's town house, he wondered if she considered the cabins adequate.

He dropped her bag on her bed and watched her perusal of the pine-paneled, plaid-curtained room. She sat on the edge of the bed that was covered in a spread that matched the curtains, and bounced a little.

"It's been such a long day," she said. "This feels comfortable."

He winced at the bold decorating. "The rooms are a little...plaid."

She nodded. "They're going for cozy. After all, their highway sign makes the claim. I like it."

So, Lady Bellows was not offended by her surroundings. He was relieved to know that—and pleased.

She lay her upper body back against the mattress and closed her eyes with a contented sigh. "I should skip dinner," she said, wriggling comfortably. "I didn't get any exercise at all today except when we ran across the terminal to catch the plane."

"Lunch was a long time ago," he said, glancing

at his watch. "And it's almost seven. You should eat something, then you can sleep."

She gave him a mildly scolding glance as she sat up. "Tell me you're not going to try to police my food intake as well as everything else."

"I'm not policing anything," he insisted, offering her a hand up. "But if you've been given a month off to restore yourself after your ordeal in the mountains, you should take advantage of the opportunity. Good food and lots of rest."

"Food doesn't appeal to me. I haven't expended any energy."

She'd taken the hand he offered but still sat there, arguing, and he had to concentrate on her words one at a time to distract himself from the feel of her small, cool hand in his.

"The sign says they serve breakfast all day," he remembered, privately congratulating himself on thinking clearly. "You could have an omelette or fruit."

She considered those possibilities and used his hand to pull herself up. He had to apply almost no counterweight.

"Maybe I'll just have dessert," she said, snatching up her purse and heading for the door.

They talked companionably for an hour over the fruit salad she finally decided upon and the steak and salad that was his reward for a trying day.

They talked about their fathers, about people in the neighborhood both remembered, and encapsulated the past twenty years for each other.

Maggie spoke mostly about her career, about the roles she'd enjoyed and those she'd agonized over, the casts that had been fun to work with and those that had been difficult.

"Did you ever expect," he asked, fascinated by her stories, "that you'd achieve such success?"

"It's funny." She shrugged, studying a section of mandarin orange on the tip of her fork. "I've loved the work, and there's such an excitement in really finding the character and giving it all you've got. So I was about ten years into it when I realized that I was a respected actress. People recognized me on the street or in the market. It was flattering."

"Did that every get to be intrusive?"

"Usually not," she replied. "I mean, if I ever ran into Sean Connery on the street, I'd run up to him and tell him I adored him and ask him to sign my grocery list. But sometimes when we were out as a family and just wanted some private time, it would get in the way. Harry was always very patient about it, but I know he sometimes wished I clerked in a store."

She stiffened suddenly, apparently surprising herself with that mention of her husband. She'd clearly put the subject of her husband and children off-limits. She ate the orange section, then asked him abruptly, "You've never been married, if I remember correctly?"

"That's right," he replied. "I came close once though, but she left me for Justin Hoyt."

She looked surprised. "The rock star?"

"Right."

"You traveled in those circles?"

"Indirectly. I provided security for them."

"Was she another celebrity?"

He shook his head. "Lisa worked for me. She was beautiful and elegant and could drop a man twice her size in five seconds." He grinned as he sipped at an iced coffee. "I thought she was remarkable."

"What happened?"

He used to remember every word she'd said when she told him she was leaving with Hoyt, but the memory of that night and a lot of his other memories of her had slipped away from him. He thought he still remembered the best part of their time together.

"She never really explained. I can only conclude he was more exciting than I am. Providing protection for people is very serious work. You can't allow yourself to be distracted like everyone else at a party or a social function. You have to be watching at all times."

She frowned. "It must be hard to hold yourself apart like that."

He nodded. "You get used to it. You just put a lid on that part of you that wants to respond and save it for later."

"But if she worked for you, certainly she understood that."

"She was in love. I guess that takes precedence over understanding and common sense."

"Did it work out for them?"

"They're still together. Though every once in a

while there's something in the celebrity news about them having a public argument.''

"I'm sorry," she said gravely. "It must be hard to have invested a part of your life in someone and have them walk away like that."

"Actually," he said, holding out his cup as the waitress came by with the coffeepot, "I got the children, so I feel very fortunate."

He was about to put the hot coffee to his lips when he saw the sudden horror in her face and stopped. "What?" he asked warily.

Children! He had children? She had to get out of here. She stifled the urge to get up immediately and run. She had to be calm so he would listen to her. But she didn't feel calm.

"You never mentioned that you had children." Her voice sounded high and defensive. She cleared her throat and tried to express herself reasonably. "In all our soul-baring exchanges of our past and present lives," she said, aware that she was failing miserably at even pretending to sound calm, "you never once mentioned children. How many do you have?"

His eyes had narrowed on her, and she suspected he wasn't angry but simply trying to understand her reaction. "Two," he replied succinctly. "Boys."

"God," she breathed in a whisper. Two *boys!* She couldn't do this. He had to take her to the airport.

"I'm afraid that changes everything," she said, gathering up her purse and sweater. "I have to go." She stood and headed for the door, half expecting him to follow and demand an explanation.

He didn't. At the door she turned to see him taking care of the check, then he followed her at a leisurely pace. Of course. He had no reason to panic. He had the car keys and she had no money to call for other transportation.

Her panic deepened as she realized the difficulty she faced.

She waited outside for him, knowing she had no way out of this without his cooperation. She would have to explain.

He pushed his way out of the restaurant, saw her standing in the middle of the parking lot and went to join her.

"I'm sorry," she said abruptly. "You must think I'm insane."

He walked toward the cabins and she kept pace, having to move more quickly than she was used to to keep up. "No need to apologize," he said. "I think I understand."

She looked up at him in surprise, noticing absently that the warm night was redolent with the smell of wildflowers and early summer. "You do?"

Hands in his pockets, he glanced at her with an understanding smile and kept walking. "Yes. You lost two boys and that's been a difficult adjustment. So you manage by never being around children. Just as you manage the loss of your husband by working all the time—and with a man who has no interest in women."

For a moment she was speechless, surprised and a little irritated that he'd guessed that about her. Then she realized it meant she might be able to get him on her side.

She smiled with relief. "I'm so glad you understand. If you'll just take me to the airport in Manchester in the morning, I'll explain to my father..."

He stopped her in front of her door, his expression regretful but firm. "I can't do that, I'm sorry. I promised your father—"

"He isn't here!" she said, her momentary calm and relief exploding into anguish. "I can not go home with you. I promise I'll explain to him that it was all my doing, that you insisted but I refused to cooperate. He knows how I can be."

Duffy smiled and nodded. She waited hopefully.

"He also knows how I can be," he said, taking her key from her slack fingers and opening her door. "I'm not taking you to the airport, Maggie. You're coming home with me, and you'll live through it. My boys are only four and seven, and while they're loud and a little reckless, they're sweet kids. You'll like them."

I *had* sweet kids, she thought. I can't do this. I don't want to do this. Then she remembered that she was a good actress.

"Please," she said in a tremulous voice, the right note of need in it. "My profession makes me sensitive and a little high strung, so it's been a little harder for me to...to find my feet again after the accident." She paused, and drew a breath that suggested how hard it was to go on. She never traded on that—at least, not deliberately. But this stubborn man required desperate measures. "And I've just been through a lot with the kidnapping. Forcing me to do something I'm really not prepared for would…"

"Maggie." He took her chin between his thumb and forefinger and pinched it gently. "I can't imagine the pain of your loss. All I know is that your father doesn't want you to be alone while he's gone, and I promised that you wouldn't be. Meanwhile, I have to get back to my boys. They do without me a lot in the winter, but during the summer I devote myself to them. We have to go home."

She could see that arguing with him would be futile. On one level she admired and supported his devotion to his children. But on another level—that of her own self-preservation—she couldn't let it destroy the only way she'd found she could function.

"Okay," she said finally. "Thanks for dinner. Good night."

He studied her a moment, and she knew he was suspecting this disagreement couldn't be over so easily. She forced a small smile to try to convince him otherwise. Then she closed the door.

She paced the carpet beside her bed, wondering what to do. There had to be a solution. There was always a solution. No one was going to force her out of her cocoon. It was miserably uncomfortable but it allowed her to function.

"I'm going to Arlington," she told herself aloud, like an affirmation that would help her visualize her freedom from Duffy's plan.

Then it occurred to her that all she had to do was get the keys to the car.

The fact that they were in the pocket of Duffy's pants was not insurmountable.

Chapter Four

She waited until 1:00 a.m. so that he would be sleepy when she asked for his help and less likely to suspect her plan. She put on a cotton robe that matched her pajamas and wrapped lightly on his door.

She was poised to knock a second time, certain she'd have to wake him out of a deep sleep, when he pulled the door open. He was surprisingly fresh looking, bare-chested and wearing blue pin-striped pajama bottoms. She should have remembered his preference for a naked torso when sleeping. His broad shoulders and nicely defined pectoral muscles snagged her attention for a moment, then she looked up into his eyes to see that ever-ready, ever-watchful expression there.

She turned on the sweetness. "I'm sorry, Duffy," she said earnestly. "I know it's been a long day for you, too, but I remembered my allergy medicine at the last minute when I packed, so it isn't in my makeup bag with all my other stuff but in the pocket of my tote, which is in the trunk."

He pulled his door open wide and stepped aside to let her in. "Have a seat. I'll get it for you."

"No!" She added a smile the moment she realized she'd said that too urgently. "You don't even have a shirt on. Just give me the keys and I'll get it."

She watched him fight a grin and wondered what that meant when he reached to the bedside table for the tab of keys the rental company had given him, removed the door key from the ring and handed it to her, putting the ignition key back.

She maintained her smile, thanked him sweetly, then went to the car and made a pretense of searching for her bag, cursing him all the while for second-guessing her intentions and squelching them.

She'd gotten this far, she thought. She wasn't going to let him stop her. She clutched a bottle of vitamins in her hand that would pass for her pills unless he asked to see them, held them up triumphantly, then closed the door, careful not to lock it.

She went back to Duffy's room to hand him the key. "Thanks," she said with an appreciative smile. "One more thing, then I promise not to bother you again."

He returned her smile. "No bother. Though I hoped you were knocking on my door at 1:00 a.m. for a reason other than the car key."

She was surprised and flustered enough by that remark to be distracted from her purpose. But only for an instant. Since she didn't know how to respond to that, she ignored it.

She pointed to the television across the room.

"Can I borrow your TV schedule? I don't seem to have one."

"Sure." He turned his back to her to walk toward it and she swept around and snatched the ignition key off the bedside table. She was facing him and smiling when he turned with the guide to hand it to her.

"Thanks so much," she said. Her eyes were snagged by that sweet, indulgent tolerance she found so impressive in him. She stared into them a moment longer, the nuclear winter of emotion she'd suffered since the accident thawing fractionally. Then she thanked him again and pulled the door closed before he could melt her icy heart any further.

She waited until 2:00 a.m. to make her escape. Fully dressed and packed, she stepped quietly out of her room into the blackness dispelled only by the bright neon of the sign advertising the cabins. She moved carefully, remembering a small step down off the walk, a row of concrete parking bumpers to be stepped over.

She tried to open the door she'd left unlocked, but it wouldn't give. She fumbled with the keys, found the one for the door, and inserted it with a small sense of exhilaration. She was almost on her way to the airport and Arlington!

A sudden deafening alarm startled her into jumping back and screaming. The indoor lights went on and the headlights flashed on and off while the urgent sound went on and on.

She turned toward the cabins and saw Duffy standing in his doorway. In the light flooding from his room, she saw that he had pulled on a shirt, probably anticipating her attempted escape. He stood with his arms folded and finally walked to the car, reached to the steering column, and the awful noise stopped.

Lights went on up and down the row of cabins, and guests were peeking out from behind drapes or stepping out of their rooms to see what had happened.

Maggie wanted to die. But that feeling wasn't new to her.

Ignoring everyone, Duffy included, she went to her cabin door and turned the knob, bumping her nose against the door when it didn't open. She tried again. It had locked behind her, and she'd left her key inside. And the manager was not among the curious who'd come out to see what had happened.

Without saying a word, Duffy held his cabin door open.

"We apologize," he said to the guests who'd stepped out in their nightclothes. "She couldn't sleep and thought she'd busy herself packing the car. She forgot about the alarm."

A small stout woman in a loud fleece robe pointed to her and said on a note of wonder as Maggie tried to disappear into Duffy's room, "You're Maggie Lawton!"

Maggie never ignored a fan, even in her own distress.

She took a step toward the woman to shake her

hand. "Yes, I am. I'm so sorry I woke you. Please forgive me."

"Oh, sweetie, you could play cymbals over my bed and I wouldn't mind! I'll never forget you in *A Doll's House*. Lenny and I saw it when we were visiting our daughter. She works in the American Consulate in London. You're so wonderful on the stage. You help us endure." She squeezed her hands. "Bless you."

"Good night," Duffy said. Maggie felt him take her arm and draw her back into his room. "We apologize again."

You help us endure. Maggie was always astonished by the degree to which an audience was affected by an actor's work. Her fan mail was filled with examples of how laughing at one of her comedic performances sustained someone or that watching her struggle to achieve or survive in a serious role made the audience want to achieve and survive.

"That's a heavy responsibility," Duffy said, taking the purse and train case she still carried and putting them aside. "Having to inspire and enlighten. And amuse."

She sat on the corner of his bed, suddenly very, very tired. In fact, she was too tired to pretend. "If they could take away the role and see the real me, they'd be disappointed. I'm all tears and cowardice."

"I remember when you were brave." He went to the head of the bed. She heard him smoothing sheets and fluffing pillows. "That kind of courage doesn't just disappear. I think if you would face your loss, it'd be there to get you through.''

''I face it every morning,'' she said with a sigh, pushing herself to her feet. ''What are you doing?''

He pointed to the bed. ''You can have it. I'll take a pillow and the extra blanket and sleep on the floor.''

''No, I'll sit up.''

''Maggie, it's too late to argue. Take the bed.''

She was surprised that he wasn't angry at having his sleep disturbed—twice—while she'd done her best to thwart his plans and put her own in motion.

''I was trying to get to the airport,'' she said, feeling as though the situation required an explanation, even if he didn't ask for one.

He nodded once. ''I figured you might. That's why I locked the door you left open and set the alarm.''

''Oh, dear,'' she said with a sigh. ''On the stage, it's considered a lack of experience to telegraph your moves.''

''In real life,'' he countered, ''it's perfectly acceptable. Especially if you're traveling with someone who appreciates knowing where you are and what you're up to.''

She watched him fold a blanket in two on the floor near the foot of the bed, then put his pillow down. ''You're amazingly even tempered,'' she observed.

''Anger gets in the way of vigilance. But I'm liable to wake up cranky if I don't get some sleep.''

''My pajamas,'' she said, ''are in the bag you left in the car when you locked it again.''

He lay down in the envelope formed by the blanket and tucked the top half around him. "You can sleep naked or in your undies or fully dressed if you like. I'm going to sleep. Get the light, will you?"

Maggie flipped the wall switch, and the room fell into complete blackness. She walked straight toward the bed, climbed in and prepared to stare at the ceiling until dawn.

But an overpowering languor took over her when she settled into the pillow. Duffy's scent clung to it, and it was somehow comforting. And, curiously at odds with her determined efforts to escape to the airport and Arlington, she liked the fact that he was just feet away from her.

That concerned her a little, but she was too exhausted to try to think it through. She closed her eyes and went to sleep.

Duffy awoke to a blow to his chest. It wasn't entirely dark but the room was still filled with shadows. He heard a shout and a cry and surfaced from a silky dream to feel bare flesh sprawled across him. He caught a whiff of a floral scent and knew the attack perpetrated on him in his sleep was not a threat but an accident.

At least not a threat to his life.

His body was in grave danger and reacted in several ways to make sure he was aware of it.

He lay quietly as Maggie struggled to get to her knees.

"Bad sense of direction?" he asked, reaching out to try to help, and connecting with bare flesh. He put both hands back on the floor and let her struggle. She'd apparently chosen the ''get naked'' option for going to sleep that he'd suggested.

She made a small sound of disgust. ''Oh, I forgot where I was, took off in the direction of my bathroom at home, and...I'm sorry.''

She was having some problem getting to her feet. She now knelt astride him and seemed to have one of her feet caught in his blanket. He knew it was boorish of him to enjoy it, but he did. As his eyes adjusted to the very dim light, he caught a glimpse of scalloped white and concluded she'd chosen the ''undies'' option rather than the ''get naked.'' Bad luck.

''Can I do anything to help?'' he asked, now afraid to move. His body was rioting, and he knew she was already embarrassed.

''My...toe's caught,'' she said, her tone mortified, ''in the blanket binding. I...can't...reach it!''

''Okay, hold on.'' Holding her upper body to him, he sat up, manfully ignoring the fact that she sat atop him, found her knee and gently, even clinically traced it to her foot where he found that her toe had either found a tear in the blanket binding or created one when she fell on him.

He freed the toe.

For reasons he didn't understand but welcomed, she didn't move. He felt her silky bare legs against his side just as he'd dreamed. His hand was splayed against her bare back, and her fragrant hair shrouded both their faces. Her elbow bit into his shoulder where she braced herself, a hand over her eyes. He felt surrounded by her, embraced by her, as though his dreams had come to life.

"I'm sorry," she said again.

He moved a hand behind him to support them and lowered her hand with the other. Her eyes were limpid and wary, her breathing suddenly shallow. The lace of her bra rose and fell against his chest.

"Don't be," he said, brushing her forehead with his lips. He felt her small intake of breath and kissed the curve of her cheek. Feeling her hand tighten slightly on his shoulder, he moved his lips to hers and kissed her gently, though a fire raged inside him. He knew this for the delicate moment it was.

She responded tentatively for half a heartbeat, then pushed him backward so that his head hit the floor with a thunk and she scrambled clear of him and ran to the bathroom.

He lay there, his head aching, and congratulated himself on his magical way with women.

IN THE BATHROOM Maggie yanked her bag in through the half-open door and closed it again quickly, certain Duffy's trek to the restaurant for coffee wouldn't take nearly long enough.

"Maggie, Maggie!" she moaned at herself as she pulled on beige cotton pants and a long-sleeved yellow sweater. "What is *wrong* with you!"

"Apparently, things we don't even want to think about!" she replied to herself as she wondered what the jail sentence was for playing footsie with the kid you once baby-sat. "You haven't been able to look at a man with *any* degree of sexual interest, much less sexual enthusiasm, and now you're kissing Duffy March! The boy you made cookies for and helped with his homework!"

Okay, he wasn't much of a boy anymore. He was all man and then some, but he was still almost ten years her junior and…and he had children!

"Ohh!" she groaned again as she heard the cabin door open and close.

"Hey!" Duffy shouted. "Do I get a turn in there? So movie stars *are* as vain as they say?"

She pushed the door open, determined to take this bull by the horns. "I'm not a movie star, I'm an actress on the stage. And I'd appreciate it if you wouldn't—" She had to take a breath and firm up her stance because he was already looking amused. "If you wouldn't…wouldn't…"

"Be under you when you fall down?" he asked helpfully.

She gave him the scolding look that deserved. "If you wouldn't get amorous with me," she finally blurted. She guessed subtlety wouldn't work with him. "I'm not looking for romance."

He handed her a paper cup of coffee. He did look wonderful this morning in a plain old pair of jeans and a red cotton sweater that dramatized his dark features.

"Maybe romance is looking for you," he suggested, toasting her with his cup. "You've been hiding long enough."

"I have not been hiding," she replied, taking a sip of the hot brew. After her long night, it was so good that she had to pause a moment while she swallowed.

"Then what have you been doing?" he challenged.

"Nothing," she replied. "I don't want that anymore."

"You don't want love anymore?" he asked as though he couldn't believe that.

"I don't want…the fuss, the chase, all the effort that goes into pairing up." She sat on the edge of the bed to enjoy the coffee, happy to hear herself say the words aloud. They were honest. True.

"At thirty-nine," he asked, looking up at her as he rooted through his suitcase, "you're giving up your womanhood?"

"Romance doesn't make a woman a woman," she informed him.

"Of course it doesn't," he agreed, "but loving and giving make her a woman. You're too young to give up the search for a man who'd want to give you love and take your love, who'd want to give you babies and a new—"

"No!" she said firmly. Then realizing she was shouting, she replied more reasonably, "No. That's over for me. Now I'm an actress and…maybe a humanitarian."

"Maggie, you make yourself sound as though you're eighty-nine," he rebuked. He had a shaving kit in his hands and a serious, concerned look on his face. "If your husband loved you as much as you claim, he wouldn't want you to enshrine yourself in his memory.''

She looked him in the eye. ''You can turn away from your past because Lisa just left you for somebody else. And you got the children. You don't know what it's like to have the people you love ripped right out of your arms. To have them gone forever, with no little faces to remind you of what you once had.'' Then she closed her eyes against the sympathy she saw in his. ''I don't mean to whine about it,'' she said, turning away to toss yesterday's clothes into the plastic laundry bag provided. ''I know I'm not the first one who's ever had such a loss. But...we were special.''

She felt his hand on her shoulder. ''I'm sure you were special,'' he said gently. ''And I'm not trying to minimize what you've endured, I'd just like to see you get to a point where you can live again.''

''I live,'' she insisted. His hand was warm and strong on her shoulder, and she didn't want to move away. ''I fill the theater every night.''

''Being someone else. You need to be able to be you.''

''That's not as desirable to me.'' She tied the top of the laundry bag in a knot and tossed it aside. Then she turned to him, determined to put an end to the subject. ''Anyway, it's my life, and I'm sure you have a lot to do, with two children and a thriving business, without worrying about it. Are you going to take that shower?''

He dropped his hand when she turned, but the

warm imprint seemed to remain. She liked that, and yet she didn't. She didn't need someone shaking up the life she'd carefully rebuilt. It was true that it was just a half life, but it was working for her.

He looked as though he had more to say but seemed to think better of it as he turned to the bathroom. He pushed the door open, then turned toward her and said with a grin, ''You want to toss me the car keys?''

She went to the bedside table for them, then back to him to slap them in his hand. ''I hope all the hot water's gone,'' she said, holding back an answering grin.

''I think we're already in it,'' he said with a wink and closed the door.

LAMPLIGHT HARBOR was located on one of the many tiny inlets on the western side of Penobscot Bay. Though Duffy had found the place quite by accident while touring New England with the boys, he'd had a sense of homecoming when he'd driven up a gravel road and spotted a rambling beach house for sale. It wasn't very old, though exposure to the elements had reduced a fresh paint job to the distressed and fortunately now-popular weathered cottage look in two years' time.

The outside was Federal in style—an odd architecture for the waterfront. But inside it was all white walls and big, overstuffed, mix-and-match furniture with wicker odds and ends and toys strewn from one end of the house to the other. He'd converted a two-car garage into a workshop for repairing old furniture and converting it into good-as-new treasures.

As he drove along U.S. 1, he found himself anxious to get there, anxious to show it to Maggie.

She was watching the tall pines that lined the road, and the occasional glimpse of ocean beyond. Sunlight played through them, birds soared and dived across the road, and a big yellow dog lazed on the scraggly front lawn of a cabin built in a shelter of trees.

"It's very beautiful," she said, smiling as she pointed to the dog. "He apparently has no plans for today."

"That's how I always feel when I come here for the summer," he said, feeling himself relax. "As though I could just sprawl in the grass and not move a muscle until someone brings me dinner."

"Does someone bring you dinner?" she asked.

He laughed. "We have a housekeeper, Desiree, who comes at noon and fixes lunch and dinner, then goes home. Sometimes, if there's business I can't escape, she stays with the boys. But her son just moved into a new house in Portland, and she went to help with the grandchildren, so she won't be back for a couple of weeks."

"Desiree's a dramatic name for a housekeeper."

"She fills it, believe me. She used to run her own lobster boat after her husband died, but her arthritis eventually got too bad and she had to sell the business to a son-in-law. Now she's happy to work for us and sell things over the Internet."

"Really? What kind of things?"

"She finds stuff at garage sales, buffs them up and resells them. We were made for each other. I pick up old furniture all over the place and fix it up, add old or new parts, repaint it. The shabby-chic trend has even simplified refurbishing. The more distressed it looks, the better."

"I love garage sales." Maggie rolled her window down and took a deep gulp of salty air. Duffy turned off the air-conditioning. "I found a Tiffany vase at one once, but Harry got upset with me because I told the woman it was valuable." She turned to Duffy to explain, a faint smile on her face. "Well, he didn't get upset, but he told me I'd never get anywhere if I pointed out the value of things to the seller. He said the point was to find bargains then turn a profit on reselling. She was a sweet little old lady, though, and I'm sure she needed the money more than we did."

"So, did she end up keeping the vase?"

"No, I have it," she replied, "but I made Harry look up the value and pay her the full amount."

He could imagine her exasperating her banker husband with that philosophy.

They passed the Welcome to Lamplight Harbor sign, featuring a young woman in a lacy white, floor-length nightgown, holding a lamp aloft, as though looking for someone.

"Population 1,257," she read. "Is the woman someone significant?"

"She's our ghost," he said. "Cathy Pruitt. Lived in the house neighboring ours. Seems her husband,

who owned a marine shop at the end of the nine-
teenth century, went to sea after they quarreled about
a woman he was seeing. He died in a gale off
Gloucester, and the legend is that she walks the
beach, still expecting him to come home.''

''Had he been unfaithful?''

''Yes. Polly Miller, the girl he'd been seeing, left
town with a baby right after he died.''

''Then, why on earth is Cathy still looking for
him?'' she asked.

He laughed softly. ''I think we put a romantic spin
on it for the tourists, but maybe it's because she
wants revenge.''

Brightly painted houses and well-kept lawns decorated with driftwood and fishnet floats signaled their
entry into town. They passed the Catholic church first
with its white clapboard structure, tall spire and pan-
sies clustered around the stairway. Next came the
Lamplight Inn, the Lobster Pot Restaurant, two
dozen shops of every description, a good half of them
antique boutiques. Maggie leaned forward as they
passed.

''We'll get you back to town to check out the
shops,'' he promised.

''Actually,'' she said with a sigh, sitting back, ''I
haven't been shopping since…in a long time.''

Since the accident. ''Then it's time. I'm looking
for an oar or a harpoon or anything long to put over
an arrangement over the fireplace. You can help *me*
shop.''

Downtown was cluttered with tourists in colorful

garb. Lobster-shaped balloons danced in the air, tied to children's wrists or fingers. The tourists moved from shop to shop, many of them wearing Lamplight Harbor sweatshirts in various colors.

They passed a modern Baptist Church, a very Gothic-looking Episcopal Church, a fish market, an ice-cream shop, then a park dotted with blankets and people picnicking, reading, resting.

"This reminds me of Europe," she said, smiling as they passed a large group of children screaming their delight at the antics of a fuzzy black puppy. "Laid out before such things as zoning laws existed." Trees crowded the road again and she turned to look back. "Was that it?"

"That was it," he confirmed. "We live about a quarter of a mile out."

"You must hate to go back to Manhattan when summer's over," she said with a wistful sigh. "It's such a pretty little place."

He nodded. "I've been thinking about finding a solution to that soon," he said. "If not this year, then next. Mike's starting to worry about me, and that's not good."

SHE DIDN'T WANT TO KNOW who Mike was, but she guessed he must be one of Duffy's boys. And if she was going to have to stay with him and his children until her father returned from overseas, she was going to have to be polite. She would happily bedevil Duffy but never his children.

"One of your boys?" she asked, hoping he wouldn't elaborate too much.

"My oldest," he said with a smiling glance filled with pride. "He's seven. He used to be okay with my work, but now that he's getting older, he worries."

"He must have been worried when you went to get me," she speculated, hating that she'd been responsible for a child's fears.

"He worries that I'll get shot." He slowed for the turn onto Blueberry Road. "But I remind him that I have a Kevlar vest and I'm usually supported by smart, quick-thinking people who are as good at what they do as I am."

"Oh, God, and you did get shot!"

"Hardly. I don't even notice it."

"Still…"

"Just don't mention it."

"You think it's a good idea to lie to him?"

"I won't lie, I just won't mention it."

They bounced a little over a gravel road between clusters of poppies and a wild white flower she couldn't identify. She saw the back of a white house up ahead, a white picket fence in the old style like spear points surrounding a yard filled with playground equipment and edged with colorful flowers. A pergola covered in pink climbing roses led the way into the backyard.

"How beautiful!" she exclaimed, unable to keep delight out of her voice.

"Thank you," he said, pulling into a gravel drive

beside the house. He parked behind a red Jeep. "My neighbor helped me put it in and, fortunately for me, does what has to be done to it in the winter. She's vice president of the Garden Society, so I'm in good hands."

"We had a beautiful garden in Devon," she said, then hated herself immediately for bringing that image to her mind. They'd had so many happy times there when she'd been between plays that she never let herself think about it. She'd sold it immediately after the accident, never able to go back to the old cottage with its rambling pale-pink roses.

"Here they come," he said unnecessarily as the back door of the house swung open with a bang and shouts of "Dad! Daddy!" rang in the air. He turned to her in concern. "They're loud and sometimes they're rude, though it's usually just youthful ignorance. You going to be okay?"

She didn't think so, but they wouldn't have to know it. They were beautiful; she could see that already. The older one had thick, stick-straight dark hair and bright, black eyes, the younger one had almost platinum-blond hair with bright, blue eyes. He could have been hers.

Pain ripped right into her, but she drew a breath as the boys peered into the car, desperate to get to their father, nosily studying her.

"I'm fine," she lied breathlessly and pushed her door open.

Duffy got down on one knee to embrace both boys, who hugged him fiercely and talked over each other to tell him about a fire in the kitchen that morning.

"Grandpa got the paper towel too close to the burner, and it caught fire!" the older boy said. Maggie remembered that he was Mike.

"Then it caught the hot pad on fire!" the little one reported. She couldn't remember if they'd gotten to his name. "Then Grandpa put it out with cake mix."

Mike rolled his eyes. "That was baking soda."

The little one shrugged. "It looked like cake mix."

"We had to help him clean up," Mike said, "but then he took us for ice cream, so it wasn't so bad. Is that the lady you rescued?" He pointed at Maggie, then apparently remembering that was bad manners, caught his pointing hand in the other and twisted them shyly.

"Yes, it is," Duffy said, standing and beckoning Maggie closer. "Maggie, I'd like you to meet my sons." He tapped the dark head leaning close to him. "This is Michael." Then he tapped the curly blond head. "And Adam. He's four. Guys, this is Maggie Lawton."

"I'm seven," Mike said, taking the hand she offered and shaking it. "I can swim really far, but only when somebody's with me. And I can climb trees, only, I'm not supposed to jump down on account of because I broke my leg last time."

"Well, that seems like a good reason to me." Studying him closely now, she saw that he bore no resemblance to Duffy. He had high cheekbones, one beautiful square front tooth and the bud of another and glossy black hair. He was very obviously of Native American descent, but Duffy hadn't mentioned that Lisa was. And the smaller boy was as different from Mike as night from day.

"And you know what?"

"What?"

"I'm gonna be a fireman. It's too bad I wasn't one already when Grandpa caught the kitchen on fire."

She gave him a hug—she couldn't help herself. It was an instinctive reaction, but the moment he was in her arms, she realized her mistake. She felt the soft baby skin, the silk of his hair against her cheek, the smell of boy.

She felt an instant's panic, then said in a whisper because her voice was choked behind a closed throat, "It's nice to meet you, Mike."

Then she moved on to the little one, who waited expectantly.

"I have a frog in the laundry room," Adam said, catching her hand. "You wanna see?" He dragged her toward the back door without waiting for an answer.

"Ah, Adam…" Duffy began, frowning worriedly as he looked into her face.

"It's okay," she whispered in that same strangled voice and followed him into the laundry room where there was a very large frog in a tub half-filled with water. A lily pad had been placed on an overturned sandpail in the corner of the sink.

"His name's Barney," he said. "Even though he isn't purple, it's a good name."

"Yeah, but what if he's a girl?" Mike, who'd followed them in, reached a hand in to pet the frog. It croaked. "It could be, we don't know. Even Grandpa doesn't know. Maybe Dad knows. Hey, Dad!"

"Yeah?" Duffy came into the room with three bags and put them down in a corner.

"Can you tell if the frog's a boy or a girl?" Mike asked, pulling his father closer. "I mean, it's not like they have boobs, or anything, so it's hard to know."

Duffy's eyes met Maggie's across the tub, and she found herself smiling at the amusement in them. She was able to breathe, she noticed, and even swallow. She was going to live through meeting his boys after all.

"No, I don't know how to tell," he said, "but we'll look it up after dinner and see what we can find out. Where'd you get him...or her?"

"We found him in the yard," Mike replied. "He seems to like it here."

"What do you feed him?"

"We got dead flies from the bug zapper." They beamed with pride over their resourcefulness.

"You still okay?" Duffy asked Maggie with a wince.

She nodded, taking one of the bags from him as he collected them again. She turned to follow him into the kitchen, then saw his father standing in the doorway.

Another challenge to her composure struck her

forcefully in the chest. Duffy put the bags down again.

Charlie March was several inches shorter than Duffy and also dark in coloring, though his hair had turned to gray. He looked strong and fit as he wrapped his arms around his son in welcome.

He'd been a handsome man in his early forties when she'd cared for Duffy, and he'd always been kind and generous to her. They'd been good neighbors to her parents, and both families had spent a lot of time in each other's homes.

"Hey, Dad!" Duffy said, slapping his father's back. "Look who I've brought home." He reached behind him to draw Maggie closer and took the bag from her.

She walked into Charlie's arms and struggled to keep herself together.

"Thank God you're safe." He finally held her at arm's length and studied her, as though looking for injury. "You must be ready for a good long rest. I'm sorry your father was called away. That's not a very nice homecoming, is it? He wired you some money, though, to help tide you over."

He was talking quickly, probably a little overcome with his son's safe return and her appearance. Even Duffy raised an eyebrow at him.

"Well," she replied. "I'm very glad it's over."

"The boys helped me get the guest room ready," he said. "You'll have to let me know if I've forgotten anything."

"Was that before or after you set fire to the

kitchen?'' Duffy asked, moving past his father and heading for the stairs. Charlie followed, taking Maggie's arm, and the boys trailed after them.

"Mike and Adam were being a little dramatic. I burned one paper towel and the thumb off an oven mit. That's hardly a four-alarmer. I'll replace the oven mit."

"Just teasing, Dad," Duffy said as they cleared the top of the stairs. He turned into a room on the right and left his bag on a dark-blue bedspread. The walls were papered in a gold and dark-blue plaid.

The boys followed him in and leaped onto the bed while Maggie and Charlie waited in the doorway.

"What'd you bring us?" Adam asked, peering anxiously into the bag as Duffy opened it.

Maggie watched the proceedings with a certain investment in the outcome. She'd been with Duffy when he'd bought their gifts at the airport yesterday morning.

"I think I forgot to bring you anything," he said, pulling things out of the bag until he revealed two brightly wrapped boxes with French script on them. "Oh, wait! Maybe I didn't."

"You never forget," Mike said excitedly. "What is it?"

The boys ripped into the boxes. Adam uncovered a bright-yellow model of a sports car, and Mike, a metallic-blue biplane.

Adam immediately pushed his car along the "road" of piping on Duffy's bedspread while Mike leaped off the bed, the airplane held aloft, and ran into the hallway, making airplane motor noises.

"What'd you bring me?" Charlie teased.

Duffy unzipped a pocket on the front of the bag and reached in to pull out a T-shirt with the Eiffel Tower emblazoned on it in gold.

Charlie looked delighted. "Thank you, son."

"Sure, Dad. Thanks for watching the kids."

"My pleasure. They're very little trouble unless one of them gets cranky." He grinned at his son. "Then they're just like you are when you've been crossed."

Maggie couldn't imagine that. Both the boy she remembered and the man she was coming to know had the most even disposition she'd ever seen. There'd been evidence of a stubborn streak a mile wide, but no sign of ill temper.

"Proof that it isn't wise to cross me," he said with a laugh. "Come on, Maggie. We'll show you your room."

He walked her to the far end of the hall where a very large room stretched the width of it. It was furnished in an eclectic collection of pieces, a fussy brass bed with a violet-patterned bedspread that matched the sheer curtains, a wicker love seat and coffee table in front of a window, a French desk across the room with a flowered settee beside it, and a gray oak armoire.

She went to open it and found a television and stereo.

"Your clothes go in here," he said, moving to

what appeared to be a wall of drawers, but were really the doors of a walk-in closet.

He pushed open another door in the corner, revealing a small but very adequate bathroom. "The tub's a Jacuzzi," he said.

"Mike put fresh towels in the closet," Charlie said, "and Adam picked the flowers." A little vase of dandelions stood on the pale-green counter.

"Everything looks perfect," she said, a little concerned that she didn't really hate being here, and that she didn't mind the boys chasing each other through the room—Adam's car rather miraculously taking flight in pursuit of Mike's plane. It did hurt a little to look at them, because they brought to mind her own boys and the thought of all their potential lost to the world and to her.

But they were also so adorable that in spite of her pain it was somehow good to lay eyes on them. They seemed so happy, so comfortable in their world. She did wonder, though, why the one had such different physical characteristics from the other.

"I got muffeleta from the deli when I took the boys for ice cream," Charlie said. "And I was in the process of making salad when you came home. I can have lunch ready if you give me about half an hour."

"Deal," Duffy said. "Maggie, I'll bring up your other bag and your train case. Why don't you sack out for half an hour. You didn't get much sleep last night."

"Well…can't I do something to help in the kitchen?" she asked Charlie.

He teased her with wide eyes. "Big stars don't cook, do they?"

"I cooked for my family...every weekend." There she went again, she thought dispiritedly. After almost two years of conscientiously never mentioning her husband and children, she was suddenly bringing them up all the time. "I'm not brilliant," she went on, pretending she hadn't noticed her own pause, "but I'm not too bad."

"Everything's done, really," Charlie said. "I just have to set the table, finish the salad. You'd be better employed resting until lunch. I'll be leaving in the morning, then Duffy will need all the help he can get."

"Can't *you* cook?" she asked Duffy.

"He can," his father replied before he could, "but he's likely to make blueberry pancakes for dinner and hamburgers for breakfast."

"So the menu's unorthodox," Duffy said, crossing the room to open her window slightly. He tugged on the shades to show her they were there. Warm, fragrant air wafted through. "We're on vacation. You're supposed to let the wildness take control when you're on vacation. Come on, Dad. I'll leave your bags by the door, Maggie."

"Great. Thanks."

Duffy closed the door behind him and his father, and Maggie sank onto the bed without bothering to hang up her things. She felt as though she'd fought a battle single-handedly and she still wasn't sure if she'd won or lost.

Her heart was beating a little quickly. She felt great and awful, hopeful, and yet worried that she felt hopeful.

She didn't know what was happening to her. It was unfamiliar and unexpected, and it was making her tired.

She welcomed the thought of half an hour uninterrupted. The bedspread was smooth and cool under her cheek, the breeze smelled of salt and wildflowers and fluttered the curtains, and the sun filled her room with light. She felt no inclination to pull down the shades.

She closed her eyes, getting a fleeting image of the night before, when the car alarm had gone off in her ear, waking everyone, then this morning when she'd fallen over Duffy in the dark.

Her heartbeat quickened, but only for an instant. She was too tired to get too excited about anything. And why would she get excited about Duffy March, anyway? She was ten years older than he was.

Well…eight.

Chapter Five

As Charlie and the boys put lunch on the table, Duffy went upstairs to tell Maggie it was ready. Noticing that her bags still stood in the hall in front of her door, he rapped lightly and called her name. She didn't answer.

When she didn't respond to a second call, he turned the knob carefully and, pushing the door open slightly, said her name again. There was still no response.

Now a little concerned, he pushed the door open farther and saw her curled in the middle of the bed, fast asleep. She seemed a little more relaxed than she'd been the past few days, though she still tended to huddle, knees pulled up, head bent down—as though shielding herself from something. It wasn't hard to figure out what that was.

He went to the foot of the bed where his father had placed an extra blanket and opened it out over her, drawing it up to cover her shoulders.

She smiled in her sleep. ''Thank you, Harry,'' she murmured.

"I'm not Harry," he whispered to her sleeping form. "And I'm just going to hang around until the day comes when that's all right with you."

With a little sound that was hard to interpret, she turned away from him, curled onto her other side and clutched the blanket to her. She sighed again, kicked once, then huddled up in a ball.

"Fine," he said softly, readjusting the blanket so that it covered her back. "Turn away from me all you want. It won't change anything."

He hauled her bags quietly inside and placed them near the wardrobe, then went to join his family for lunch.

"MAGGIE'S REALLY PRETTY," Mike said as he and Adam and Duffy stood in line at the Beachside Bakery. Charlie was making spaghetti for dinner and needed a loaf of Italian bread for garlic toast. "How long's she gonna stay?"

"Until her father comes home," Duffy replied, moving up one space as a woman left the shop with a cake box balanced on the palm of her hand.

"That's Elliott, right?"

"Right."

"Well..." Mike was frowning, clearly confused. "You mean, she can't stay by herself without her dad? But she's a grown-up."

Adam, hanging on to Duffy's hand, was jumping up and down, and Duffy gave him a gentle yank to stop him. "This is a shop," he reminded quietly. "Not a trampoline, okay?"

"Okay, but when we get there—" he looked at the display case of several dozen types of tempting treats "—can I have that rolly thing with the chocolate in it?"

A chocolate cream horn. One of Duffy's favorites. "Sure. But I'd like you to be still until we get there."

"Okay. Only two in front of us!" Adam held up three fingers.

Duffy pushed one finger down. "That's two." Then he turned his attention back to Mike. "It's not that she can't be left alone because she wouldn't know how to take care of herself. It's because she's had a lot of sad and scary things happen to her, and we don't want her to have too much time to think about them. And that can happen when you're alone."

"Yeah," he replied knowledgeably. "Grandpa said her little boys died in an accident."

"Yes. On a train."

"I thought people only died when they were old, but Grandpa said sometimes those things happen and nobody can explain it. It's just the way it is."

"Grandpa's very smart."

"What would you do if me and Adam died on a train?"

I'd die myself, he thought. Aloud he said, "I'd be very, very lonely. Just like Maggie is. But even though it's true that those things happen and there's nothing we can do about it, they don't happen to everyone. Lots of people go their whole lives and nothing awful like that ever happens. So, I don't want you to worry, okay?''

''Okay.'' Mike stepped up with him as he finally moved to the head of the line. His eyes greedily perused the case, the heavy matter of life and death apparently forgotten in the face of pastry. A healthy perspective for a seven-year-old, Duffy decided.

Since Mike's choice for a treat was also a chocolate cream roll, Duffy bought half a dozen of them, as well as the loaf of Italian bread. They climbed into his red Jeep and headed home.

MAGGIE AWOKE WITH A START, aware of billowing curtains she didn't recognize and a beautiful airy room that was completely unfamiliar. Wait. She put a hand to her head, as memory penetrated her slow-starting brain.

This was Duffy's house. In Maine. She was staying with him until her father returned.

As always happened when she awoke, the hopeful first instant of every new day was quickly squelched by her grief. She let herself think about that for a moment, deal with the brutal reality of it and the fact that her life was irrevocably changed. Then she watched the curtain strewn with violets puff into her room with that delicious salty air and felt, probably for the very first time, an uneasy attempt to accept it.

It startled her into getting to her feet and looking for something to wear. Lunch, she remembered. Muffeleta and salad. She had to hurry. She wasn't sure how long she'd been asleep. She hadn't reset her watch since coming to the States, and she saw no bedside clock.

She dug into her case, found capris and a matching shirt in pale green and pulled them on. Then she brushed her hair, wrapped it into a knot and hurried downstairs.

She found the table set and Charlie stirring something very aromatic in a pot. She moved closer and leaned over his shoulder to look.

"Hey, Sleeping Beauty," he said. "How're you feeling?"

"Very well," she replied. She pointed to what looked like pasta sauce. "I thought you said you'd bought muffeleta."

He balanced the spoon on the side of the pan and turned to give her an indulgent smile. "That was lunch," he said, moving to a corner of the counter where a garlic bulb rested on a cutting board. "This is dinner."

She scanned the walls for a clock and found a very antique-looking one on a wall near the phone. It read 5:18.

"Ohh, no," she said with a hand to her mouth. "I'm so sorry. I had no idea I'd slept so long. I haven't reset my watch and…"

"No need to apologize." Charlie handed her a cube of butter and a small glass bowl. "Want to put that in the microwave for me, please? Wait!" He went to a closet in the laundry room and returned with a blue and white-striped apron. "Put that on."

"Thank you." She tightened the neck strap, then folded up the waist to make it fit and tied it. "Melted or just soft?"

"Just soft," he said. "For garlic spread."

She popped the butter in the microwave and set the timer. "Want me to slice the bread?" she asked.

"As soon as Duffy and the boys get home with it." He pointed to the refrigerator. "There's a bottle of Johannesberg Riesling in there. Pour yourself a glass. I know you're supposed to drink Chianti with spaghetti, but I don't like it, so I bought Riesling. Glasses are in the cupboard right beside it."

"Works for me." She found the bottle on its side on the second shelf. It had already been opened and was topped with a decorative wooden stopper.

The microwave dinged and she went to get him the butter.

Then she poured two glasses of wine and placed one beside him on the counter. She climbed onto a nearby stool and sipped at her wine as she watched him work. When she'd baby-sat Duffy, his father had often prepared something for them to eat just before taking off for the evening. This was pleasantly familiar.

"I can't believe," she said, "that here we are after all those years in between."

He smiled at her as he crushed a garlic clove with the back of a wicked-looking knife. "Isn't it nice to know that relationships can span time and separation?"

She nodded. "Yes, it is."

''Your father's so pleased that you came home with Duffy,'' he said. ''He was afraid you wouldn't.''

''You spoke to him?''

''He called while you were asleep, but he asked me not to wake you. He was taking a break from a meeting.''

''I didn't want to come,'' she admitted, ''but your son's a stickler for his commitment to his clients. He insisted he'd made a deal with Dad that he would deliver me into his hands, and he was adamant that he intended to do just that.'' She made a rueful little sound. ''Like I'm some helpless little thing.''

''Fathers always worry,'' he explained, putting the knife aside to sip at his wine. ''It's less to do with how capable you are and more with our need to know you're safe.''

She frowned. ''Duffy's work must make you crazy.''

''It does,'' he agreed. ''The only comfort in it is that he's so competent. Of course, that wouldn't save him if fate chose to intervene.''

''Then, you must be happy he's thinking about doing something else.''

Charlie lowered his glass to the counter in surprise. ''He is?''

Oh-oh. ''Um…well, he said something about…''

''What did he say, exactly?''

She sighed and slumped in her chair. ''Oh, Charlie, I'm sorry. I thought he'd told you, or I wouldn't have…''

He raised a hand to stop her. "It's okay. Just tell me what he said. Quickly, before he comes home."

"Just that Mike has started to worry about him, and he doesn't like that."

He nodded. "He's been afraid Duffy will get shot. He talked about it a few times while Duffy was gone."

Maggie nodded. "So he's thinking about doing something else."

"What?"

"He didn't say."

"Did he say when?"

"This year, or next year at the latest." She took a big sip of her wine. "I am sorry. That's the kind of thing you should have heard from him."

"Don't worry." He smiled and picked up the knife again. "I won't say anything. I'm good with secrets. And I'm glad he's concerned with Mike's feelings. In my day the job and supporting your family was everything. Today the kind of father you are isn't related to how good a living you make. Though Duff's doing all right there, too."

"The boys seem very happy," she observed.

"They are," he agreed. "Taking Lisa up on her offer was the smartest thing Duff ever did—for all of them."

"Her offer?" Maggie asked, wondering if she had the right to enquire. Of course, if Charlie didn't want to answer, he didn't have to.

But he seemed to have no such reluctance. "Did he tell you about Lisa?"

''Only that they had a relationship, and when she left, he got the children.''

He glanced up at her with an expression that told her there was a lot more to the story. He put the knife down and picked up his wine.

''It's a little more complicated than that. She already had Mike when she moved in with Duff. His father was an artist she took up with in Sedona. She stayed with Duff for about a year, then she fell for that rocker and followed him, taking Mike, who was three. She came back not quite a year later with a three-month-old baby—Adam. Apparently the rocker didn't like kids and they were getting married, so she wanted to know if Duffy wanted his son.''

Maggie listened in open-mouthed astonishment. She couldn't imagine such a careless dismissal of one's child.

''When he said he did,'' Charlie went on, taking another sip of his wine, ''she told him he could have Adam without contestation on her part if he'd take Mike, too. Apparently, his father didn't want him.''

''My God.''

''Yeah. Duff had always treated Mike like his own and missed him when Lisa left. So he was happy to take him.''

''My God,'' she said again.

''I'll trust *you* to keep that secret,'' Charlie said. ''It's clear when you look at the boys that their backgrounds are different, but Duff never bothers to explain. And as far as he's concerned, they're both his.''

"They're certainly a lucky pair."

The words had just left her lips when they burst into the kitchen, Mike carrying a pink bakery box and Adam, a long loaf of bread he was using as a baton as he marched around the kitchen.

"Look, Grandpa, I'm in a parade!" he exclaimed.

Mike sidled up to Maggie and held the lid slightly open so she could see the contents. "Look what we bought!"

"Yum!" she said.

Duffy came toward her, then sidetracked to rescue the bread before Adam twirled it as he threatened to do.

"Okay, let me have that," he said. "I'm sure Grandpa would prefer it didn't fall on the floor."

"I was gonna catch it," Adam assured him.

"Well, this way you don't have to. Go wash your hands for dinner. You, too, Mike."

Mike put the box in the middle of the table. To Maggie he said, "Make sure Dad doesn't eat my cream roll. He keeps saying he's gonna."

"I'll guard it with my life," Maggie promised.

The boys scampered off.

"That was some nap," Duffy said, coming to stand near her as he passed his father the bread. "You all right?"

She wasn't sure she was. There was a little fluttering going on in her chest, a strange sort of tension in her at his nearness. And now when she looked up at him, she knew that he'd claimed his son from a woman who hadn't cared about him and rescued another child to boot. So he wasn't simply a man who took action against physical danger, but he had a moral compass, too.

The tenuous attraction that had been building since the Pyrenees, despite her effort to ignore and then discourage it, suddenly swelled with a life of its own.

Oh, God, she thought worriedly. She was too old for a crush, because that was all it could ever be.

"I'm fine," she said, pretending she really was. "I got lots of rest, but I'm sorry I missed the muffeleta. Want a glass of wine?"

"Please." He leaned a hip against the counter near where Charlie worked. "Mike insisted we save your piece. You can have it for a midnight snack, or something. He's taken quite a liking to you."

She retrieved another glass, half filled it with wine and handed it to him. She felt flustered and silly, and not betraying that was difficult.

"He's a sweet child," she said, making a production of capping the bottle. He was watching her and she wondered if he could feel the tension in her. To try to make him believe she wasn't affected by him, she teased, "You know, like you used to be before you grew up into a hardheaded man."

Charlie laughed.

"You're calling me hardheaded?" he asked, leaning conspiratorially toward his father. "Did she tell you she stole the rental car keys and tried to strand me in New Hampshire while she drove home to Arlington?"

Charlie looked up, grinning. "No! What happened?"

"He'd set the car alarm," she explained, relaxing a little at the humorous note the conversation had taken. At least, it was humorous now. Last night she hadn't been so sure. "About gave me a stroke."

Charlie crowed. "Relationships are so much more interesting when you're evenly matched," he said, then added, as though just realizing what he'd said, "Not that you have a relationship, but the potential is there. I mean…you know…a single woman, an available man." He looked from one surprised face to the other and said abruptly, "Never mind. One of you put the coffee on, and the other preheat the oven for me. I can't keep chitchating like this and get dinner ready, too."

THIS WAS GOING TO BE harder than he'd anticipated, Duffy thought as he tried not to notice Maggie sitting in the middle of the sofa with the boys crowded in on either side of her. She was looking up information on frogs so they could determine Barney's gender.

Her hair was wound into a loose knot, spiked ends of it sticking up and out in an artlessly charming manner. She looked soft and vulnerable in the lamplight, and he'd heard more of her laughter in the last hour than he had in the past three days.

The woman who'd been so adamantly against coming home with him because she hadn't wanted to spend time with his children, had won them over completely in a very short amount of time.

And Duffy himself was a complete goner.

The three of them laughed loudly together over something and he lost all ability to focus on the bills he tried to organize at the desk in a corner of the room.

"That means the female—that's the girl," Maggie explained to Adam, "is bigger than the male. That's the boy."

"But, if we don't have a boy *and* a girl," Mike pointed out, "we won't know which one is bigger. Maybe we need to catch another one." He sounded excited by that solution.

"Well, let's see if there's another way to tell." Maggie kept reading. "Okay, here it says, 'the male is also distinguished by expansible vocal sacs on the neck or throat that serve as resonators for the mating call. Females are ordinarily nearly mute and have no mating call.'"

"What does *that* mean?" Adam asked.

"Mute means something can't talk," Mike said. "So that means the girl frogs can't talk?"

Duffy couldn't help himself. "Mute women?" he asked, looking up from the desk. "That must be another planet."

"Men puffing themselves up and asking women to mate?" she countered, looking at him reproachfully over Adam's head. "No, I think it's this planet."

Grinning, he went back to the bills and tried again to focus.

He was shocked when the clock struck nine and Mike told Maggie that it was their bedtime.

"You have to read us a story," Adam said. "Then you have to kiss us and make sure we're nice and warm, then turn out the lights."

Duffy felt her panic before he even looked up and saw it. Meeting his children hadn't been as hurtful to her memories as she'd thought, but tucking them into bed might be more than she could deal with.

He pushed away from the desk. "Guys, Maggie has some things she has to do tonight," he said, going to join them. "I'll tuck you in tonight, and maybe…"

"No." Her voice sounded frail. She cleared her throat and said with a little more certainty, "I can do it."

"Maggie…"

"I can do it," she insisted. "Do we need milk and cookies before we go up?"

"No." Mike bounded up and caught her hand. "Let's go."

Adam scrambled after them, racing to catch her other hand.

Duffy watched a little worriedly as they climbed the stairs, wondering if he should offer to help.

"She's experienced," his father said, noting his concern. "You should keep your old man company. I'm going home in the morning, remember?"

He was probably right, Duffy thought. If she needed help—if it got to be too much for her to tuck them in—she'd shout. She wasn't shy about telling him what was on her mind. Usually. It was what was in her heart that was the mystery.

He turned to his father, one ear still cocked to the goings-on upstairs. "You're welcome to stay, you know. It's not like you have to hurry back, except to catch your Friday-night poker game."

"Thanks, but the boys have worn me out." When Duffy frowned, wondering if something had happened that he hadn't shared, his father added quickly, "They were very good and didn't give me a moment's trouble, but they're busy every minute. Whew! That's why parents are young."

"I'll take you to the airport after breakfast."

"That'll be great. And I'll be back for Labor Day and our end-of-summer celebration."

"Good. Unless you get married between now and then."

His father blinked as they sat across from each other at the table. "What?"

"Mike told me Mrs. Venturini called you three times while I was gone."

He made a scornful sound, but he also turned a telltale shade of fuschia. "She was having trouble with her dishwasher. I always help her with it."

"So I heard. And she irons your shirts. They make shirts now that don't have to be ironed, you know. Unless, of course, you *like* Mrs. Venturini coming over with her ironing board."

He was quiet for a moment, then he looked up at Duffy, his expression serious. "I don't mind it. She's a very nice woman."

"Ah. Are you going to bring her in September?"

"Would you mind?"

"Of course not."

His father smiled. "Good. I'll bring her."

Duffy got up to pour coffee just as Maggie came down the stairs. She had a smile in place, but she was pale.

She dusted off her hands, pretending, he was sure, that tucking in the boys had been easy. "Mission accomplished," she said. "Would it be all right if I went to bed early? I promise to be more useful around here tomorrow, but today I don't seem to be able to keep my eyes open."

"Of course." She'd stopped halfway down the stairs, and Duffy went to the foot. "You need anything?"

She shook her head. "No. My room's very comfortable. Why don't I make breakfast? I make a great French-toast-and-sausage casserole. I saw eggs and milk in the fridge. Do you have sausage?"

Duffy nodded. "I'll take it out of the freezer tonight. But Dad's leaving early…"

"I'll be up early," she promised.

The last thing he wanted at that moment was for her to disappear upstairs. Unless he could disappear with her. But he knew this was going to take time.

"Okay," he said. "Good night, then. If you decide you do need anything, you know where my room is."

That could have been construed as suggestive and he wasn't entirely sure he hadn't meant it to be—but she apparently suspected nothing and simply smiled and said good-night.

Charlie smiled at him as he resumed his chair. ''Bet you wouldn't mind if Maggie set up her ironing board here.''

Chapter Six

It was shortly after 3:00 a.m. when Duffy heard the stairs creak. He was stretched out on the sofa in sweat bottoms and a T-shirt, unable to sleep. He felt jumpy—not a good quality in a bodyguard. Fortunately, he was a bodyguard on vacation.

He couldn't account for the uncharacteristic case of nerves, unless he could blame jet lag or unresolved desire. He was seldom a victim of his feelings, but he certainly seemed to be tonight.

Entertaining dreams of Maggie Lawton all those years had been one thing. Having her in his home, only yards away from his room, was quite another. He'd come downstairs shortly after midnight to put a little distance between them.

He sat up, wondering if one of his boys was having a problem. But he dismissed that thought as soon as it formed. If that had been the case, either one of them would have come thumping down the stairs, "Daaaaad!" running ahead of him at high volume like a siren.

And it wasn't his father because he could hear him snoring from down here.

That left Maggie.

He braced himself, swung his feet to the floor and went to the kitchen doorway to be a good host.

The refrigerator door was open and she was visible to him in the light from inside as she turned, something caught between her teeth. She had the jug of milk in one hand and closed the door with the other. Her hair was down and disheveled, and she was wearing the sweater he'd put on her in the Pyrenees. About an inch of a nightshirt showed below it and everything else was shapely leg.

Her name caught in his throat as he tried to alert her that he was there.

And that was probably fortunate because she managed to cross the few steps to the table before spotting him, so that when she screamed and dropped the jug of milk and the slice of muffeleta in her teeth, they fell onto a place mat. She snatched up the milk quickly and stared at him with a hand to her heart.

"You scared me!" she accused.

"Sorry," he said, flipping on the light. "I thought you might be having a problem."

She rolled her eyes at that and smiled ruefully. "When am I *not* having a problem lately?"

He went to the cupboard to get her a glass and pulled down two.

"So you are?"

"No." She sounded growly, then sighed and filled the glasses with milk. Then she sat down and he joined her. "I've just slept enough. And I was lying there, wondering what I'm doing here. I should be home working."

"You need a break."

"I thrive on work."

He disliked people who told other people what they should think or feel, or otherwise analyzed them when they could usually use a little analysis themselves. But he had an important stake in her attitude, and he was certain she was playing tricks on herself.

"You're hiding in the work, Maggie," he said gently. "When you're being someone else, you don't have to deal with the reality of what's happened to you."

She met his eyes and she looked more hurt than annoyed. He hated himself, but this was important.

"Do you think I'm that much of a mystery to myself that I don't know that?" she asked, tearing the Muffeleta in half and handing him a piece. Now he really hated himself. "I want to forget. I want to pretend it didn't happen. I want to play the heart and soul of another woman because mine are in shreds. So what? It prevents me from leaping into the Thames."

"I'm sure diversion's useful for a while," he said. "But the day's coming when you're going to have to look your loss in the eye and start over."

"Why?" she asked baldly. "I'm all right."

"No, you're not," he corrected. "You're afraid of men and children. Is that any way for a woman to live?" He didn't have to explain what he meant.

She blinked at him. "I read Mike and Adam a story, didn't I?" she demanded quietly. "I tucked them in."

"But you were pale afterward," he insisted, "and you had to go to bed." He put his piece of muffeleta down on a napkin and thought about how best to say what he had to tell her next. There was no good way to put it. "I think it was so hard for you because you like the boys, and you know they like you. You're drawn to them. I think you're even drawn to me. And you're resisting that, because if you admit it you think it compromises your devotion to your husband and children."

"Duffy, I have nothing to admit," she said with what appeared to be complete conviction. "I'm not enshrining myself with my family as you put it yesterday morning, but I'll never be able to put them aside to make another life for myself."

"I understand your love, Maggie," he said reasonably. "But you can't dedicate yourself to a family that's gone. It's a waste of your considerable talents as a woman. It's fine to give love generously, but if it's never returned, you'll atrophy. And the stage won't do it for you forever. Eventually you'll need to really feel love and laughter, not just make it up for an audience."

She'd taken a bite of her midnight snack and chewed and swallowed while she raised a superior eyebrow at him. "A lot you know about the theater," she said finally. "All the emotion we project is genuine."

"Where does it come from?" he asked.

"From our own experiences," she replied.

He had her. "Then, where is it going to come from, from now on, if you're never going to have any? Will the simple memory of an emotion be strong enough? Doesn't it have to renew itself to give you the power all the critics rave about?"

OF COURSE IT WOULD. Wouldn't it? She took another bite of muffeleta, pretending the question hadn't shaken her.

She'd been so full of emotion the past two years, portraying love, anger, grief had been easy. But... would it grow more difficult as time went on? Humor and laughter had been harder to portray, but she'd thought that had simply been because there'd been so little in her life since the accident.

But, wasn't that his point?

"I'll find it," she said simply, popping the last bite into her mouth and getting it down with milk. Her throat was dry. "Why are you down here, anyway?" she asked, maintaining her mask of unconcern. "What's keeping you awake?"

"You," he replied. "I've been in love with you for a long time."

"Puppy love," she said, hoping to dismiss it and his notion of it by being mercilessly honest.

It didn't appear to be working. He simply shook his head and said amiably, "The puppy's now a big, bad dog. Watch yourself, Maggie. I'm coming after you."

"God!" She stood in complete exasperation. "Am I talking to the wind or are you deaf?"

"Both, I think," he replied.

"Good night, then," she said, putting her glass on the counter and dusting off her hands. "There seems to be little point in this conversation."

"That's what I've been telling you."

She hurried upstairs, climbed back into bed and pulled the blanket up over her head, then remembered that she'd promised to be down early to fix breakfast. Thanks to her mention of her room's lack of an alarm clock, one had magically appeared sometime that evening. It read 3:42. She picked it up and set it for 6:00 a.m. That didn't leave her much time for sleeping, but she'd probably had twelve hours already today. She should be fresh by early morning.

Though what she was going to do about Duffy she didn't know. Murder was promising, but there were the boys to think about. Maiming would be satisfying. She'd have to give it some thought. She pulled her blankets up again and was surprised to find herself exhausted once again. This "restful" vacation with Duffy was going to make her old before her time.

Funny, though. For the past two years, she thought it *was* her time to grow old. Now...she didn't know what she thought. She didn't know anything about anything.

THE BOYS LOVED HER CASSEROLE, despite their sadness over the fact that Barney had escaped when

Adam opened the back door. Duffy comforted them with the promise of a more traditional pet when the time was right.

"When is that?" Mike asked.

"Soon," Duffy promised noncommittally.

The entire nine-by-thirteen baking pan was empty before Maggie was halfway through hers. She served everyone more fruit and apologized that there wasn't more.

Charlie shook his head. "I wouldn't have time to eat more. I have to be back in Arlington for a meeting at eleven. My plane's supposed to be refueled and ready to go by nine."

"You won't crash, will you Grandpa?" Mike asked worriedly.

"Absolutely not," Charlie said with complete confidence. "I'm a very good pilot, and I'm always very careful."

"Call us when you get in," Duffy said. "Even if you're late for your meeting."

"I will." Charlie got up from the table and excused himself. "Wonderful breakfast, Maggie. If you ever decide to give up the stage and want to hire on as personal chef to a charming old gentleman…"

"And who would that be?" Duffy interrupted.

"Grandpa means him!" Mike said seriously, pointing to his grandfather, unaware his father was teasing.

Duffy pretended surprise. "Really? He confused me with the charming part."

"Funny, son," Charlie headed for the stairs.

"What is 'charming'?" Mike wanted to know.

"Ah..." Duffy considered his answer while taking a sip of coffee. "It's being nice and pleasing in a way that makes people do what you want them to do."

"But Grandpa's not that way?"

Duffy laughed. "Yeah, he is. I was just teasing him."

"If Maggie was his chef...that's a cook, right?"

"Right."

"Well, if she was his chef, we could see her every time we visited him."

"But Maggie's a great actress in England," he explained. "He was teasing, too, when he said that about her being his cook. A lot of people go to the theater just to see her."

Maggie stacked plates and tried to pretend she wasn't being discussed. Then Mike lured her into the conversation, anyway.

"But, if you like to cook," he said, catching her arm as she reached across him for his fruit bowl, "you could be a great actress *and* cook for somebody, couldn't you?"

"I suppose I could," she admitted. "But what I really want is someone to cook for *me*."

"Daddy cooks really good!" Adam said, a dashing milk mustache decorating his upper lip. "If you came to live with us, he could cook for you, too! Couldn'tcha, Daddy?"

Duffy's eyes met hers, lively with amusement. "I could."

She had to look away from those eyes. The charm he'd just explained to Mike was in them, as well as a predatory gleam that revved her pulse and left her curiously flustered. She hadn't been flustered in more than a decade.

"That's you, Duffy," she said, turning her back to him as she took a stack of dishes to the counter. "Always cooking up something."

He was silent for a moment, then she heard him say, "Okay, guys. Let's pitch in and help Maggie."

CHARLIE HUGGED EVERYONE before he left, including Maggie.

"Don't forget to bring Mrs. Venturini when you come back," Duffy said.

"Who's that?" Maggie asked as they watched him climb into a little Cessna.

"His lady friend," Duffy replied. "Sounds like he's really interested in her."

"Ohh," she said, delighted to know Charlie had a romance underway. "Love is in the air?"

"Everywhere you turn," he said.

She looked up at him to see if he'd directed that remark to her, but he had lifted Adam into his arms and was answering a question about another small plane taking off.

They waited until Charlie was airborne before they moved away from the window.

"Okay," Duffy said to the boys. "What do you say we show Maggie downtown Lamplight Harbor?"

"Yeah!" Mike took heartily to the plan. "When we go downtown, we always go to the bakery!"

"Or for an ice cream!" Adam said. "Can we have both, Daddy?"

"Maybe, but not at the same time. Maggie? Want to walk around downtown before the streets are too thick with tourists?"

She did, but she didn't want him to think he had to entertain her. "Don't you have things you have to do?"

He spread both arms out to indicate his freedom. "I'm on vacation. I got an e-mail from my assistant this morning telling me they're doing fine without me."

"That's probably comforting to know," she said, "if you're planning to—" She stopped herself before she could say more than she should in front of the boys, as she'd done to his father. "You know," she ended lamely.

It took him a minute to follow her, then he smiled. "That's true. But from the standpoint of having a sense of your own indispensability, it's demoralizing."

Each boy had him by a hand and was pulling on him. "You're indispensable to them," she said, indicating the boys with a jut of her chin. "That should perk you up."

He grinned as the boys dragged him off and she followed. "My goal is to be indispensable to you, too."

She let that pass, thinking as she trailed them out

to the parking lot that she was already a little too interested in him despite her claims to the contrary.

"How's the situation overseas?" she asked as they climbed into the car and buckled up. "I didn't see the morning paper."

"I couldn't find anything about it," he replied, looking over his shoulder to check the boys, then turning on the motor and backing out of one of the parking spots in front of the airport's tiny terminal. "Apparently your dad called yesterday while you were asleep and the boys and I were gone."

"Yes. Well, I guess worrying about him won't accomplish anything." She looked out the window at black-and-white cows munching on grass, a tree-dotted slope behind them going down to the ocean. "When I'm working and don't have time to wonder how he's doing, it's easier for me to forget he's on a dangerous assignment."

"I'm sure he'll try to call again. And stop thinking about work. You're supposed to be resting. Did you bring a bathing suit?"

"No," she replied. "Our vacations were usually spent on a farm. No swimming."

"Water's a little cold here for swimming, but we do a lot of sunbathing. The boys like to play in the sand. We'll have to buy you one."

"Please." She wanted to squelch that idea. "I could be going home tomorrow for all we know, and I haven't seen myself in a bathing suit since right after Morgan was born, and that was pretty traumatic for me. Nothing was quite where I remembered it was."

He laughed lightly. "Well, everything appears to be in the right place now. And all that vitamin D from the sun will be good for you. Help you get stronger."

"I'm strong," she disputed. "And probably also very, very white."

"We've got sunscreen."

"That's not what I mean. I just don't want to be seen."

"It's a private beach," he insisted. "And it's time you stopped hiding."

The inclination to punch him in the eye was almost overpowering, but he *was* driving and there *were* two little boys in the back seat. She settled for a verbal punch. "If this were a play," she said, "I'd have you disposed of in act two."

"If this were a play," he replied, turning onto the busy little road that led into town, "I'd have already seduced you, and you'd be thinking of ways to hold on to me rather than get rid of me."

She was just a little shaken by that bold claim. "Well, fortunately it's not a play."

"No, it's not. No one's writing you out of this, Maggie. You have to come to the happy ending all by yourself."

DOWNTOWN LAMPLIGHT HARBOR was just awakening, a few shoppers already out strolling. Sandwich-board signs on the sunny sidewalk announced sales inside the shops. Shopkeepers opened their doors and swept their sidewalks, calling greetings to one another. Flags and banners fluttered, and the sun picked out the hoods of cars, the window of a brass shop filled with nautical trinkets and Adam's hair. Maggie found herself stroking his curls as she and the boys stood on the sidewalk, waiting for Duffy to join them.

The architecture was very different from her London neighborhood, of course, but the sense of bustling commerce, of a little community allied for the common good was very much in evidence. Tempting aromas from the bakery drifted by on a light breeze.

Maggie stopped, letting the sun beat down on her, and got lost in the moment. There was poignant memory in it, but also something very immediate, too: the sun on her face, the feel of a child's silky hair under her hand, life going on around her, then a man coming toward her with an easy, confident stride—not just toward her but into her space, very present, very vibrant.

She felt almost as if she'd been injected with some sort of stimulant. Everything in her body seemed to crank up a notch—pulse, perception, even…hope.

She felt her lips part in surprise, and her jaw might have fallen open if Duffy hadn't caught it between his thumb and index finger. Hope. She hadn't felt hope in two years.

He stared at her, probably wondering why she was standing there like a statue in the middle of the sidewalk. His eyes tried to read hers, but apparently unable, moved down to her lips.

Her head tipped back and her body reached up. She wouldn't be able to deny that later. The pull of his kiss was there even before he made a move, and she wanted it more than anything.

Duffy couldn't account for that infinitesimal inclination of her body toward his, but he took advantage of it before she could think and change her mind. Reminding himself that the boys were watching, he put a hand to the back of her head and lowered his mouth to hers. Passion, desire, long years of dreaming of her rose to demand so much more than they could share in the middle of a downtown sidewalk, but he banked the yearning and strove to express instead the tenderness of his admiration. Then he lengthened the kiss one more moment to let her know he had so much more to tell her when she would be willing to listen.

She didn't pull away. She didn't gasp indignantly when he raised his head. She didn't turn on her heel.

She stood there, looking into his eyes, her own reflecting a wary confusion. He'd shaken her conviction that her life was over. That was good enough for him. For now.

He saw the boys share a giggle.

Duffy pointed to a shop halfway up the block with its old-fashioned symbol sign. Only, this one boasted a red-and-white polka-dot bikini. ''Alice's Beachwear,'' he said, ''is right there. I'll keep the boys busy and we can meet you...''

"I want to go with Maggie," Mike said, his arm looped in hers.

Adam, jumping up and down with his excitement in the sunny day, said, "Me, too. Me, too. Me, too!"

Duffy looked from one boy to the other in surprise. "You don't want to come with me to the toy store?"

"Can't we all go *after* Maggie buys her bathing suit?" Adam bargained.

"I'll come and meet you there," Maggie said. "And I won't take long, I promise."

Mike shook his head. "No."

Adam, still jumping, said, "No."

Duffy, realizing what an ace in the hole he had in his boys falling in love with Maggie, shrugged helplessly. "Okay. I guess if I'm not going to be *lonely...*" He emphasized the word as he made a theatrical attempt to look pathetic.

Mike caught his hand with his free one. "You can come with us!"

Maggie barely withheld a grin. "That was just a little too close to melodrama. Your performance lacks subtlety."

"Thank you," he said. "I'll remember that."

Duffy kept the boys busy in the play equipment part of the store while Maggie tried on bathing suits, but he found himself distracted, his eyes veering toward the triple mirror in the corner where she occasionally appeared to check on the fit of a suit.

Mike was picking out a beach ball from a large bin, and Adam had chosen a tin bucket and spade and tried it out in the small sandbox on the edge of the department. Duffy heard Maggie's voice and turned—and felt all the air leave his lungs.

She stood in front of the triple mirror, a clerk holding out some kind of sheer cover-up jacket sort of thing standing aside as Maggie turned.

But all Duffy could see was Maggie. The suit she wore was a simple light blue, a one-piece with no midriff showing and no bold exposure of breasts, though there was a slight but tantalizing mounding of flesh above the scalloped top. The fabric, very thin and supple, seemed to sweep across her from one side to gather in a ripple of fabric on the other, as though cinched there. It was cut high on the sides so that her long, slender legs went on and on.

She hadn't noticed him and turned to look at her reflection over her shoulder. Then she turned to the mirror again and he got the most delicious sight of the back of the suit that dipped down to her waist and showed off her very shapely bottom.

The clerk helped her on with the cover-up, a transparent thing that would keep the sun off without concealing what was underneath.

She turned again and saw him. He leaned an elbow on a nearby counter to try to look casual and because he needed the support.

The clerk looked to him for an opinion.

He had to clear his throat. "Pretty," he said simply.

She disappeared inside the fitting rooms but he didn't seem to be able to move.

"Da-ad!"

Mike's shout brought Duffy out of his trance. He guessed by the sound of the boy's voice that that shout wasn't his first attempt to get his attention.

"What?" he asked.

Mike pointed over Duffy's shoulder.

Duffy turned to find Adam standing in the display window among the mannequins, collecting starfish in his bucket. Several early shoppers had gathered to watch.

God! Duffy scooped him out of the window, put the starfish back, then went to the counter as Maggie approached from the dressing room, running a hand through her disheveled hair.

The cashier held up his Visa. "I have your husband's credit card," she said. She took the ball and bucket the boys handed her.

He saw Maggie debate with herself whether or not to try to correct the woman, then decide against it. She seemed to be willing to concede this one to him. "Nothing for you?" she asked.

"I got my gift," he replied, signing the slip, "when you tried on the suit."

Chapter Seven

They were on their way to the toy shop when they ran into Judy Douglas, Duffy's neighbor. She was a tall brunette with a mother-earth freshness about her he'd always admired. She wore no makeup, did little with her hair except tie it up with a clip, but he'd always thought her beautiful. She wore a tank top and a long silky skirt. In each arm was a flower pot filled with a plant with green-and-white leaves.

"You'll have to check out the nursery!" she said excitedly. "Hostas are on sale." The boys greeted her warmly, then she noticed Maggie. A pot clutched to her, she stuck her hand out in the warm, open way she dealt with everyone and everything.

"Judy Douglas," she said. "I'm Duffy's neighbor." Then she seemed to notice something and said with a perplexed tilt of her head, "You look familiar."

"Judy, this is Maggie Lawton," Duffy said, surprised to notice a very slight stiffening in Maggie's manner, though she took Judy's hand and smiled politely. "Maggie's an actress."

Judy nodded, as though just remembering that. "In London. When I was at Oxford, I saw you in *Barefoot in the Park*. Wow. You're something else."

Maggie hitched a shoulder modestly. "Thank you. Corie's a clever, funny role. It's hard to mess up."

"I doubt that. What are you doing with this character?" Judy inclined her head in Duffy's direction.

"Our parents…" she began, then shifted her weight and started over. "We were neighbors as children and…" Curiously, she didn't seem to know where to go with the explanation.

"She's visiting," Duffy said simply. "Judy's the one who takes care of our place all winter."

"Speaking of which," Judy said. "I've been meaning to talk to you about the fund-raiser for the library. Do you have just one minute?"

Adam was jumping up and down and Mike was staring longingly in the direction of the toy store. When Maggie said, "Why don't the boys and I go on, and you two can talk without interruption," he thought it was a good idea—except for the uncharacteristically sweet note in her voice that suggested she was covering up another emotion entirely. She couldn't be jealous. That was just too much to hope for.

She smiled with every evidence of courtesy at Judy, then took off down the street, the boys attached to her like little leeches, Adam bouncing like Tigger.

"Beautiful woman," Judy said. "Made me laugh like a fool in that play, as I recall." Then she observed without preamble, "You're in love."

He refocused on her with a smile. "Yeah."

"She doesn't want to be. Got a little bubble around her."

"She lost her husband and children in an accident. She thinks her life's over."

A line appeared on Judy's brow. "How sad. Well, if anyone can convince her that isn't true, it's Mike and Adam. Now. About the benefit auction…"

Judy secured his donation of a chair, then spotted another neighbor she'd wanted to approach about it, thanked Duffy, wished him luck with Maggie, and moved on.

As he started toward the toy shop, he saw two men walk out of it, followed by his boys. Now *both* boys were jumping up and down. One clerk carried a sit-in truck with pedals. It was painted bright red and had several boxes in the back.

The other clerk carried a bright-green airplane that he had to hold sideways because of the wingspan. He placed it on the sidewalk, and Mike climbed into it. Again, people gathered to watch.

The car had a horn that Adam pressed repeatedly, giggling with delight at the loud *ooga* noise. Mike's plane made a motor noise Duffy suspected would eventually drive him crazy, but that seemed to thrill his son. The boys loved the attention from the passersby and took it as encouragement to race up and down the street. Duffy thanked heaven for the early hour and the sparse foot traffic.

"What have you *done?*" he demanded of Maggie when he reached them. The boys had pedaled to the end of the block and were now headed back toward them, the car in the lead.

She was grinning too widely at first to respond. Adam waved at her as he pedaled like crazy, and she waved back.

"They fell in love with them," she said, looking up at him with laughter in her eyes. It waned for just an instant when she added, "They were something my boys would have loved." But her eyes ignited again as the boys passed them in a hail of horn and motor noises, headed for the other end of the block. "And it was a small way to pay you back."

The look she gave him to underline those words was filled with gratitude, but also with a devilish glint that suggested a payback of quite another kind.

"Have you thought about how we're going to get those home," he asked, gently pinching her arm, "in the back of a Jeep?"

"Yes," she replied, pinching him in return. "I thought the boys and I could wait in the bakery while you run the car and the plane home."

"Then, you realize our shopping's over because we won't have a moment's peace until we take them home to play with their new *noisy* toys?"

She nodded. "I was finished, anyway. Shall I order you a mocha or a frappuccino or something so that it's ready by the time you get back? And what kind of pastry?"

"Just coffee," he replied, putting a hand up like a traffic cop to stop the boys as they headed back toward them. "And a glazed old-fashioned. You're going to have to wear that bathing suit day and night to counteract the effects of that horn and motor.''

He explained to the boys about having to leave them with Maggie while he took their toys home. Mike didn't protest at all, and Adam, only minimally.

''Can I have a chocolate-covered donut?'' he asked. Sometimes, depending on whether or not they were going elsewhere, chocolate-covered donuts were off-limits because of the mess.

''Yes,'' Duffy replied.

''Can I have two?''

''No.''

Adam accepted the rebuff to his opportunism with good grace. ''Okay.''

''Okay. I'll be back in about ten minutes.''

Duffy got the car in the back of the Jeep, but he either had to make a second trip or tie the plane to the roof. Fortunately, Judy was just climbing into her van across the street. She believed in being prepared for anything and had all sorts of things in the back of it.

''Of course I have rope,'' she said, hauling out a formidable coil of nylon rope and handing it to him. ''Leave it on the back porch when you're done.''

''You're an angel,'' he praised.

''I know,'' she said.

A kindly passerby took the free end of the rope as Duffy tossed it over the top of the plane and helped him secure it.

''Thank you,'' he said after they'd tested the knot. ''Can I pay you back in crullers?'' He pointed to the doorway of the bakery where Maggie and the boys watched.

"No need to pay me back," the man said, sketching him a wave as he started off to catch up with his family, who'd moved on without him. "We're from Wisconsin. I had to lash three bikes to the back, find room for eleven pieces of luggage and a birdcage. I relate to your predicament. Have a nice day."

"Thanks. You, too."

"That," he heard Maggie say to the boys, "is an example of a Good Samaritan."

"Samaritan?" Mike asked. "What's that?"

"Someone who helps someone else," she explained.

"Like when Dad went to France to get you?"

Duffy didn't wait to hear her reply. He drove off thinking that she might *think* her life as a mother was over, but she seemed to act like one instinctively. And she was beginning to respond to him.

All he had to do was play it cool and let his boys be their charming selves. Sooner or later she'd realize that if she was going to let herself become attached to them, he was going to be part of the bargain.

MAGGIE'S FATHER CALLED that night after dinner. It was very early morning in his part of the world.

"Are you coming home?" she asked, half hopeful, half fearful. She was a 116-pound bundle of ambivalence.

"I'm afraid I've got a few more days' work here, sweetheart," he said. His voice was warm and comforting, the way she remembered it on stormy nights when she was a child…and the month that he'd stayed with her after the accident. She remembered hearing it through her sobs. "I'm so sorry. I know you came home only because I insisted, and then, before you even got off the plane, I was whisked away…"

"Dad, it's all right," she assured him quickly. He sounded so upset. "I'm fine. Duffy's been very kind to me, and his boys are adorable."

"You're sure you're okay?"

"I'm sure."

"When do you have to be back in London?"

"I've got a month's leave," she replied. "Hopefully, you'll be back before I've used it up?"

"I will," he promised, "if I have to go to the president."

"He came to one of my performances when he was visiting the prime minister," she laughed. "He seemed to like my Blanche DuBois. Maybe I can get you in to see him."

"Very funny."

"Daddy? Are you safe there?"

"Perfectly," he replied. "We have a detachment of marines at our beck and call. Don't worry."

"Okay, then. Hurry back. Let me know when you get to Arlington and I'll get a flight right over."

"No, you stay there," he said. "I'll stop by and pick you up. I want to thank Duffy in person for getting you back safe and sound."

"Well, he had a little help from the gendarmerie."

"Maybe. But he's the one who prevented Eduard's right-hand man from shooting you when the army attacked."

That was news to her. "He did?" She remembered being held down in the dirt, bodies thudding to the ground nearby. But she hadn't seen a thing.

"He did. Stay well, okay?"

"I will. You, too, Dad."

Maggie headed for the living room to tell Duffy about her conversation with her father and met him coming into the kitchen with a giggling boy under each arm.

"You didn't tell me," she said, wondering why it was so important that she confront him about this now, "that…that you saved me from…from…" She didn't want to say the words in front of the boys.

He raised an eyebrow as the boys laughed and wriggled. "From…? Oh." He apparently realized what she wouldn't say and put the boys down. "Mike, can you pour milk for you and Adam? Use the plastic glasses. Adam, you know where the cookies are."

Mike ran to the refrigerator for the milk, and Adam went to a drawer in a low cabinet for the cookies.

Duffy put a hand to Maggie's shoulder and pushed her gently before him into the living room. She turned in the middle of the room to face him.

"Dad said Eduard's man came to shoot me when the army attacked."

"He did."

"And you…killed him?" It was hard to force the words out. A rush of emotion blocked her throat and burned her eyes.

He looked confused by her reaction but answered her question.

"Yes."

A tear slid down her cheek and she swiped it away. Frowning, he drew her with him toward the deep sofa and sat her down beside him.

"Maggie, that's why your father sent me," he said, holding her arms as her lips trembled. "Taking a life is an awful thing, but it was him or you. I was just so grateful I reached you before he did. I saw him heading for you and knocked you down just as he took aim."

She nodded. "I heard him fall," she said on a gulp of air. "But I didn't realize…"

"I thought you didn't need to know that. I'm surprised your father told you."

She wanted to speak but didn't seem able to. He wrapped her in his arms.

"Maggie, I'm sorry," he said quietly, "but I couldn't let him…"

"No, no," she interrupted him, pulling away from him to look into his face. She had to swallow to explain. "I'm not upset that you killed him. I mean…of course I'm upset. It's awful that anyone had to die. But I'm just… I just realized that for two whole years I wanted to give up my life and join my family, but now…" Tears now rolled rapidly down her cheeks with the weight of her discovery.

''Now,'' she went on, her voice barely a whisper, ''I'm glad I'm alive.''

He brought her back to him as tears fell afresh, and she wrapped her arms around his broad middle, very happy at that moment to be there. It was a little startling to realize that she so valued her life.

She heard Mike's voice ask worriedly, ''What's the matter with Maggie?''

''Nothing bad,'' Duffy replied. ''Sometimes adults have to cry, too. Just like kids do.''

''Does she have an owie?''

''Sort of.''

''Maybe you should give her some ice cream, like you do for me and Adam?''

''That's a good idea. Can you dish some up? Use the step stool to get the ice cream, not a chair, okay?''

''Okay.'' Footsteps scampered off.

Maggie lay against Duffy's shoulder, exhausted. She hated the confusion that seemed to plague her constantly lately, and tried to sum up events so that she could assess where she stood.

''So, I owe you my life,'' she said.

He felt relaxed, one hand holding her to him, the other gently stroking her spine. ''Right,'' he replied lazily. ''I think the accepted coin of repayment is a lifetime of servitude.''

''You'd have to move to London,'' she murmured, touching her fingertip to the pattern on his shirt, ''so that I could serve you when I'm not onstage.''

''I don't mind moving to London,'' he said. ''But

you might have to give up the stage. I'm not sure I'd like the competition.''

"I'm onstage from eight to ten-thirty, except on Sunday, when there's a matinee. That would hardly interfere with my duties.''

"You must have a different concept of your indenture than I do.''

She sat up, leaning an elbow on his shoulder. She drew a deep breath, feeling it fill her with possibilities. That was something new. Or, rather, something so old she'd forgotten what it felt like.

But it simply could not involve what Duffy had in mind. She remembered telling him that before, but he seemed to have a serious problem listening to her.

"Duffy, I owe you so much,'' she said seriously, "and because of that, I want to make it absolutely clear to you that you have to stop this. You're handsome and charming and brave enough to get between me and a bullet. But I'm a lot *older* than you are, and while I'm flattered that you apparently find me attractive, I don't think we can have a serious relationship. And that's the only kind you should consider with two little children dogging your every footstep.''

"You've said that before.'' The hand that had been rubbing her back now rested comfortably on her hip.

She took it and held it in hers. "Well, if you'd pay attention, I wouldn't have to repeat myself.''

"The fact that you say the same thing over and over,'' he argued quietly, "doesn't make you right.

It just makes you repetitive. And, in this case, *wrong* over and over.''

"Says you."

"I'm the vote that counts. I'm the one you owe your life to."

"Duffy…"

Before she could try to counter his argument, Mike ran into the room with a small mixing bowl overflowing with blueberry ripple ice cream.

She kissed his cheek and pulled her hand from Duffy's so she could take the bowl, suggesting to Mike that he get a second spoon so his father could help her.

"Ohh," Duffy said as Mike ran off to the kitchen again, "another sign of impending domesticity. It's a slightly different spin on the Rockwell painting of a couple sharing one milkshake with two straws."

"She wasn't ten years older than he was," she said, dipping her spoon into the purple stuff and offering him a bite.

"Neither are you." He took the bite and swallowed. "And this is like a different spin on Eve and the apple."

She rolled her eyes at him. "I have no intention of trying to seduce you."

"That's what you say now." He took the spoon from her as Mike brought her another. "But tonight when the thunderstorm hits, you'll be wanting to climb into bed with me. I remember how you hated them. You kept telling me over and over that it was going to be all right, but even at eight years old, I knew you were trying to convince yourself and not me."

She looked up at him worriedly over the bowl. "It was a beautiful day. Not a cloud in the sky."

"I'm just passing on information from the weatherman."

She reached over the back of the sofa to push the curtains aside. Big pewter clouds were moving in on an orange sunset. She let the curtains fall again and said matter-of-factly, "I'll be fine. I got over my fear of thunder when I grew up."

He held the bowl out to her as he took another bite. "Okay. If you're not, though, you know where to find me."

DUFFY GUESSED as thunder crashed overhead just after 1:00 a.m. that Maggie hadn't been kidding about outgrowing her fear of it. The storm had begun about ten minutes ago, the sound of it loud and persistent— but there hadn't been a sound from her room. Rain fell in pounding sheets and the wind blew. He looked out his bedroom window in the direction of the water and hoped that every little boat out there had come safely home hours ago.

He went to check on the boys, who usually slept like the dead despite the noise. They were fast asleep. He covered Adam's bare foot with the edge of his blanket, then stepped out into the hall and looked in the direction of Maggie's closed door.

There was a brilliant flash of light, an immediate crash of thunder, and the few lights on in the house went out.

He heard her door burst open, and an instant later something soft and fragrant collided with him with a little scream.

"Whoa," he said on a laugh. "It's me. I was just about to check on you. Are you all right?"

"Uh…sure. Are you?" He could feel the softness of her breast against his upper arm. Her heart was pounding. And she was wearing his sweater again.

"I'm frightened," he replied, huddling against her as another clap reverberated overhead. "Will you come sit with me? Ow!"

"Oh, you are not!" she chided on a note of laughter as she punched his arm. "And for heaven's sake, remember what I told you about subtlety in your performance."

"I thought that was subtle. Wasn't that subtle?"

Thunder crashed again, and she looped her arm in his. "Doesn't matter. I'll come and sit with you if it'll make you feel better. But we should check on the boys first."

"Already done. Both fast asleep."

He led her back to his room where a tall window looked out onto the water. As he drew her inside, cautioning her against bumping the dresser on her right, a fork of lightning split the sky. She shrank back. "Geez! Would you mind closing the drapes? I've always thought a bare window invites the lightning inside."

"No, I'll do it," he said, pushing her gently until she bumped up against the mattress. "But lightning looks for height, not bare windows."

"Well…we're in the top of a two-story house."

He laughed softly as he went to close the drapes. "Yes, but there are a lot of things higher than we are. And we've got a lightning rod, anyway."

"Oh," she said simply. He judged by the location

of her voice that she was in his bed. He fought against reacting to that in the way he might if the circumstances were different. He put a hand out to touch the wall and let it lead him to the other side of the bed. The closed drapes put the room in real darkness.

"You okay?" he asked as he reached down for his pillows and propped them up against the head-board.

"Yeah," she replied. "You understand," she asked in a tentative voice, "that I just want to sit?"

"That's all I invited you to do," he reminded her.

"Yes, but you lied about being frightened."

"So did you."

He felt her foot stir somewhere beside him, then a pillow suddenly smacked him in the face. He uttered a dramatic "Oof!" of pain.

"Duffy, I'm sorry!" she exclaimed, reaching out in apology. She touched his chest, his chin, then gently patted his cheek. "I just meant to prop up my pillow."

"Yeah, that's what they all say," he teased, "then they hit you with a pillow and pretty soon they're into major sex play. I know your type."

She giggled as she settled her pillow and sat beside him. Her hip brushed his as she wriggled into place. "This happens to you all the time, does it?"

"It does and it's exhausting," he said. "So don't try to lure me into a pillow fight. I'm tired of being nothing but a source of entertainment, a—"

Thunder boomed, interrupting him. It was a slight distance away this time, but she didn't seem to notice as she looped her arm in his and leaned her head against his shoulder.

"I don't think of you as entertainment," she said.

"You don't?" he asked, disappointed.

She laughed again, then yawned. "No. I think of you as...security. Safety."

He wasn't sure he liked that. That *was* what he did, after all, but it wasn't the way he wanted to be perceived. At least, not by her. At least, not all the time.

Then, unexpectedly, she reached up and kissed his cheek. "Good night," she said. "Thank you."

"Sure," he replied.

He felt the gradual reduction of tension in her body until her weight leaned completely against him and she breathed deeply and evenly in sleep. Because he represented security to her. Safety.

Now all he had to do was sit up all night with her soft, round body leaning against his and figure out how to make her understand that considering him safe could be dangerous.

Chapter Eight

Duffy was grumpy, or so the boys told Maggie. It was noon and she had yet to see his face.

When she'd awakened that morning in his bed, he'd been so long gone that his side of the sheets were cold. She'd made a quick search for the boys and found that they, too, were gone.

Then she saw the Jeep pull up around nine-thirty, but Duffy didn't come inside. The boys trooped in with a bag from the bakery and a box of berries from the market.

"Where's your dad?" she asked Mike.

"He's helping Judy fix her roof," he replied. "He said we should eat without him. Can we have blueberry yogurt on the blueberries?"

"Yes, but you should have more than doughnuts for breakfast," she said, opening the fridge.

"Dad fixed French toast for breakfast," he reached around her for the milk, which he had to hold with both hands. "This is morning snack."

"Okay," she said, feeling guilty that she'd slept through breakfast. "You sit down and I'll wash the berries.'' Judy, huh? She remembered how warm and safe she'd felt last night during the storm, and was suddenly, curiously, violently jealous. Then she scolded herself for wanting more than she could have. Wasn't she always telling him it could never work between them?

Judy was the type of woman he should bring into his life—smiling and open and free of tragedy and baggage.

And close to his age.

"We're supposed to save him the apple fritter," Adam said.

Maggie looked down at her left hand and the fritter she held with a big bite taken out of it.

"Oh-oh," Mike said, noticing the doughnut. "Dad's grumpy. He's not gonna like that."

She remembered the gentle, understanding man of the night before and couldn't imagine he would be upset about a doughnut.

She was wrong.

The boys had long since finished lunch when he walked in shortly after one o'clock. The children were running the car and the plane up and down the back deck, horn blaring, motor noise revving.

There was an unusual tension in him, she noticed. His clothes were grubby, his hands dirty, and with his hair disheveled and a storm brewing in his eyes, he looked like a stranger.

"Can I fix you something to eat?" she asked, putting the kettle on the burner to make herself a cup of tea.

"No, thanks," he said, heading for the stairs. "Judy made me a sandwich. I'm going to shower, then I'll come down for my fritter."

She opened her mouth to confess that she'd eaten it, but he was already halfway up the stairs.

She went to sit on the sofa in the living room with her tea and a magazine, noticing that the sky was clouding over again. She stuck her head out the French doors, wondering if the boys were cold, but they'd built up such a head of steam riding back and forth that they were comfortable.

Fifteen minutes later Duffy appeared in the doorway, clean but still a stormy-eyed stranger. He made her feel just a little less secure.

"Where's the fritter?" he asked.

She lowered the magazine to her lap. "I ate it," she admitted. "I'm sorry. By the time Adam told me it was yours, I'd already taken a bite."

He turned back into the kitchen without saying a word. She put her magazine and tea on the table and got up to retrieve the bakery bag from the top of the refrigerator. She found him pouring himself a cup of coffee.

"I saved you the maple bar," she said, reaching up on tiptoe for the bag.

"Never mind," he said.

"Why? It's very…"

"I don't want it," he snapped.

She took the bag down, anyway, certain if he saw the creamy icing on the maple bar, he'd forget the fritter. When she handed it to him, praising the merits of maple, he took the bag from her and tossed it back where she'd gotten it. He started to walk out of the room with his coffee.

"Duffy!" she shouted at him. "What is the matter with you? If your pastry needs are that specific, maybe you should come home and make them clear before disappearing next door for hours!"

She had no idea where that nasty outburst came from. She was surprised to discover herself just as tense as he was.

He frowned at her and took several steps back into the room. "I was helping her with her roof," he said with exaggerated calm.

"Of course," she responded in the same tone. "You go to everyone's rescue."

His focus narrowed on her, and he put his cup down on the table. "I thought you'd decided you were *glad* I saved your life."

"I am," she said defensively, "but that doesn't mean I have to take it quietly when you're rude and awful!"

"I didn't think asking you to save me the apple fritter was so bad."

"Why didn't you take it with you to Judy's to be sure you got it?"

He raised an eyebrow at that and crossed his arms. "I thought you said you weren't interested in me."

"I'm not."

"Then why all the cracks about Judy?"

"They're not cracks. You were with Judy."

"To help her with her roof."

"So you've said. And while you were there, I inadvertently ate your apple fritter. Tough."

She could see him fight a smile. "Well. It's a good thing I didn't get too serious about you owing me your life in return for my saving it. I mean, considering you aren't even willing to save my doughnut."

She shouldn't have touched him. She knew that the instant her hands connected with his forearms. But she was so exasperated, the need to shake him superseded all clear thought.

"I didn't realize it was your doughnut!" she shouted at him, her own body being shaken more than his by her efforts. "But you're being such a jerk about it, I'll go to the bakery, pick up half a dozen more and eat them, too! In fact, I'll…"

She never got to finish the thought. The storm in his eyes seemed to collect into two hot centers as he caught her arms in a biting grip, effectively causing her to release his.

She knew instinctively what was on his mind.

She feared his kiss more than anything—and wanted it more than anything. To try to make him as confused as she was, she threatened quietly, "Don't you dare."

"Sorry," he replied, a slight twist to his mirthless smile. "It can't be all your way."

And then he kissed her. It began as a hot and demanding communication with none of the tender reassurance of the first time. This was no request to ask her what she felt, but a firm and thorough declaration of his feelings. It left her in no doubt that his arguments on behalf of their relationship were heartfelt.

And that he was angry about something. But she wasn't sure what.

He finally released her, then studied her for a moment with a look in his eyes that said that hadn't done as much for him as he'd hoped.

Okay, it had been delicious and exciting, but it had done nothing for her confusion, either.

"I don't understand what you're mad about," she said frankly.

He closed his eyes for patience, then said with a long-suffering, quiet growl, "No, you wouldn't. You're happy in your little world, determined not to care, and happy enough with that decision that you can spend most of the night in my bed and not even notice I'm there."

She knew what he meant, but she tried to pretend affront so she didn't have to deal with what he meant. "I didn't know you wanted anything last night but to offer me comfort."

He ran a hand down his face in frustration. "I didn't," he said, "but when you fell asleep all wrapped around me, the rest of the night was a little harder for me than it was for you. And that's the way it always is. You'll take comfort but nothing else. And you think that's all it ever has to be."

"Look," she said. "I didn't want to come here in the first place…"

He looked heavenward in supplication. "I know, I know. You'd have been content forever on the stage in London being somebody else so that you don't ever again have to be you. But that's acting, Maggie, that's not living, and I care too much for the gutsy girl who saved my life, to let her waste the rest of hers.''

She stood toe-to-toe with him. ''Duffy, I'm a grown woman,'' she said, pointing her finger at her chest. ''Not some sweet little thing you can charm with your muscles and the strength of your personality. You're just upset because I won't fall into line with your plans.''

''Oh, that's not the problem here and you know it,'' he said a little hotly. She was tempted to take a step back, but she held her ground. ''In fact, I'd happily fall into line with your plans, if you had any. But all you seem to want to do is ignore what you feel for me.''

''How do you know I feel *anything* for you?'' she demanded.

''Maggie! Were you just here for that kiss or not?''

He turned in exasperation—and saw Mike and Adam standing there just inside the kitchen, bony little bodies in shorts and T-shirts looking very small and very worried.

She saw him draw a breath to shift gears. ''Hi,'' he said easily. ''What's going on?''

''Why are you yelling?'' Mike asked.

''I knew you'd be mad about the fritter,'' Adam said.

He squatted down in front of them and put a hand

on each boy's arm. "I'm not mad about the fritter. We're just having a disagreement. You know how that is. You guys do it all the time. It's nothing to worry about."

Mike frowned at him. "I like it better when you're talking and laughing."

Duffy nodded and squeezed the boy's arm. "So do I. But life just can't be laughter all the time. Sometimes you get upset. How come you're not riding?"

"'Cause you were yelling."

"Okay, I'll come out and watch you ride, then there won't be any more yelling."

Maggie, feeling guilty because it had been partially her fault, though he'd taken all the blame, asked, "Can I come, too?"

Mike studied her sternly. "You promise you won't yell at my dad?" The boys were smitten with her because they weren't used to having a woman in their lives, but their love for their father ran deep.

She promised.

As the boys ran outside, now shouting gleefully at the prospect of having an audience, Maggie stopped in the doorway and turned to Duffy. "I am sorry about the fritter."

"Would you forget the damn fritter?" he said, pushing her gently out onto the deck.

THE NEXT WEEK went by in a weird state of peaceful tension. Duffy made a point of keeping his distance while still doing his best to be a good, thoughtful host, and a friend, if Maggie needed one. But he was going to have to stop offering comfort. Body-to-body contact strained his libido to an intolerable limit, and he had to think about surviving for the long haul. When the boys were occupied, he spent a lot of time in his workshop refinishing garage-sale finds he'd made over the last few years.

Elliott Lawton's overseas efforts to stabilize alliances for the purpose of forming a stable government seemed to be taking much longer than anyone expected.

"Hardheaded, self-righteous so-and-sos," he said when he called in the middle of the week to tell them things weren't going well. Maggie was putting the boys to bed, so Duffy talked to him until she came down. "Determined that nobody gives an inch to anybody for fear it'll be interpreted as weakness. Know what I mean?"

"Yes, I do." And he did. He and Maggie seemed to be engaged in the same kind of war, with no wise, understanding gentleman like Elliott to arbitrate for them.

"How's it going there?"

"We're doing fine."

There was a significant pause, then a heavy "How's Maggie?"

"Fine. We spend a little time on the beach every day so she's getting a tan. And she's sleeping well when it doesn't thunder."

"Thank goodness. I knew spending time with you would be good for her."

Maggie ran down the steps at that moment, and he held the phone out to her.

He wandered onto the deck to give her privacy, but left the French doors slightly ajar to allow him to overhear her half of the conversation. She talked a lot about things Mike and Adam had said or done, but very little about him.

He was beginning to wonder if he'd been wrong in thinking he could charm her into a relationship. He'd dreamed about her his entire life, but while he'd been living alone, she'd had an apparently erudite and loving husband, who'd given her two charming, intelligent boys. She'd had the family life he longed for, and it was entirely possible she couldn't see or didn't want that with him.

Maybe once had been everything she needed.

No. He couldn't believe that was true. She was too young and vibrant to live the rest of her life alone. But he was going to have to consider the possibility that she might want to spend it with someone else.

That was grim.

He heard her hang up the phone after a few minutes, then nothing. He sank into one of the Adirondack chairs on the deck and looked up at the stars, wondering what he would do when she went back home with Elliott. Maybe that would be good, he speculated. Maybe she'd miss him and the boys and want to come back.

He smiled grimly at the night. Self-delusion was a dangerous thing.

The French doors opened suddenly, and she came

out to join him, accompanied by the distinctive sound of ice cubes tinkling. She handed him a barrel glass.

"Wine," she said, taking the chair beside him. "And Seven-Up. It was all I could find."

"Thank you. Your father sounded well."

"Yes." She took a deep sniff of the air. "I've got another week, at least."

The words echoed inside him. Not, "My father's going to be another week," but "I've got another week, at least," as though his delay was a boon for her and she was pleased about it.

He was sure she hadn't even realized what she'd said. She leaned back in her chair and looked up at the sky—and he knew he'd acquired a whole new lease on the situation.

"This air is so pure," she said, breathing in again. "And after the rain, it's like perfume. You must miss it when you're in New York."

"I do," he admitted. "When I sell the security business, I'm going to retire here and open a shop downtown with my furniture."

"Won't you miss the excitement?"

"Maybe a little, but not the pressure. And I'll get to be around for the boys all the time. Lamplight Harbor has a good little school. Do you miss London?" he asked.

"Not as much as I'd imagined," she replied. "I miss the work, though. If I lived here, I'd have to work in summer stock or something. Start a theater company."

He turned his head sideways, his heart giving a

lurch. Keeping his voice calm was difficult but imperative. "You thinking about getting a summer place?"

"No." Her ice clinked as she took a drink. "I just meant, for the sake of our discussion, if I did live here, I'd have to have theater."

"Theater would be a nice addition to Lamplight Harbor."

"So would a handmade-furniture shop."

He said nothing more about it and neither did she. They sat side by side and finished their drinks, then said good-night.

Life went on for a few more days, the tension increasing proportionately to his determination to control it.

She seemed to grow even livelier, spent part of each day frolicking with him and the boys on the beach. They cooked outside, sought the shade of the deck in the afternoons and enjoyed the long, slow evenings with television or board games.

The boys flourished. Their devotion to her now ran deeper than the novelty of having a woman around the house who wasn't the housekeeper. They went to her with discoveries, complaints, the occasional injury.

She always gave them her full attention, arbitrated with the wisdom of obvious experience and teased them with their own silliness when they fought about inane slights and offenses.

He became more and more determined that she

was going to remain in their lives forever, if he had to raise his children in England to accomplish that.

MAGGIE WAS SURPRISED one morning when she stopped in the middle of fitting a turret on a sand castle and discovered that she was...happy. Happy!

Being hopeful had been a major giant step forward, but that had somehow morphed into...she stood still to shut out distractions and focus on what she felt. Yes. Happy!

She looked around her at the blue ocean, the laughing children, Duffy, shirtless and tanned working over the gas grill, and felt a jolt as though lightning had run through her.

Apparently feeling her stare, Duffy looked up and raised an eyebrow in question.

"What?" he called.

She shook her head. The knowledge was new and a little scary. "Nothing," she said, then, looking for an excuse that would satisfy him, she put a hand to her stomach. "Hungry!"

"Kabobs coming up," he said.

Jake and Jamie Baker, who lived on the other side of Judy, wandered over, apparently following their noses. Duffy invited them to stay, and the four boys occupied a blanket near the sand castle while she and Duffy shared a cotton throw nearby.

He smelled of salt, sand and smoke flavor, and she found herself feeling absurdly happy, free and... lustful.

She nibbled on a green pepper she'd pulled off her

kabob stick. "You're quite the outdoor chef," she said, reaching for the lemonade she'd served in water bottles with lids. She'd recycled half a dozen for the boys to use to help prevent spills. "When you open your shop, there'll probably be some quiet times during the winter. You could write a cookbook."

"The kids eat my cooking, but I'm not sure everyone would. And you don't count," he said with a wink, "because you're just discovering you have an appetite."

"You must have to keep fit to do what you do."

He agreed to that with a nod. "But I don't worry about it in the summer."

Ignoring his fitness program didn't seem to be hurting him, she noticed. He was all strong angles, muscled planes, flat stomach and long, strong legs.

Her heart fluttered. She wondered what was wrong with her. She hadn't thought much about sex in two years, much less longed for it. But it was on her mind a lot now. Today, particularly.

He tossed his empty kabob stick in the basket she'd used to carry things out from the kitchen, then surprised her by putting a hand to her cheek.

"You're not getting too much sun, are you?" he asked, reaching for the sunscreen. "You're very pink."

"I'm fine," she said, "blondes just get pinker than other people."

"Here. Sit still."

She complied as he dotted some of the cream into his palm and applied it to her cheeks with his index finger. "I'm sure if you go back to London with a tan, your director will be upset."

Go back to London. Usually she thought of home with a sense of comfort. It was close to where Harry and the boys rested, and where she'd been so happy and gained success.

To her surprise, it just seemed very far away from Duffy, Mike and Adam.

A sudden pall fell over her newfound happiness. She was going to have to choose. There was no other way to go on.

She felt Duffy's hand against her cheek suddenly. He was finished with the sunscreen—this was simple physical contact.

"I hate it when you look like that," he said, rubbing his thumb over her cheekbone. "I'm sorry I brought up London."

She held his hand to her cheek and leaned into it. "No, don't be. It isn't you. It's just the...shocking realization that it isn't home anymore. And how could that have happened in just a little over a week?"

She saw the effect of her admission in his eyes. He had to know she meant that London was no longer home because he wasn't there.

His smile came very slowly. "I'm not hearing an admission that you're falling in love?"

He looked entirely too self-satisfied. "Mike and Adam are pretty powerful stuff."

"It isn't just Mike and Adam," he challenged.

"No." Facing the choice had somehow made it

clear to her that choosing to love another man would never diminish her love for Harry and her boys. "Lamplight Harbor is quite a wonderful place."

"It isn't Lamplight Harbor," he insisted.

She turned to him, intending to persecute him further, but his eyes were so filled with love and adoration that she couldn't do it. She leaned toward him and said under the sound of gulls and little boys' laughter, "No, it isn't. I think I might be falling in love with you."

He caught her hair in a fist and pulled her to him for a swift, hard kiss. He held her close for a moment, then breathed a sigh against her ear. "I thought you'd *never* open your eyes to that."

"Well, Duffy, it's not like it's without its problems."

He straightened to look at her. "What problems? I mean, apart from the fact that we live on two different continents." He gave her a grin that meant he was amused by it but not daunted.

"You're just a…a kid," she said, "and I'm a year from middle-age."

"Okay, that's it." He got to his feet and yanked her to hers. Without warning he hauled her over his shoulder and headed for the water. She kicked and screamed in protest.

"Hey! Look at Daddy!" Adam shouted.

Soon the boys were clustered around them cheering him on. Fine, loyal children they were. Of course, she supposed that to them, being dunked in the icy water of the Atlantic was probably great fun.

"If you don't put me down!" she threatened as her upside-down view of things brought the water ever closer, "You can forget the…the nighttime's entertainment I had planned."

Apparently unimpressed with her threat, he kept walking.

"Duffy!" she shrieked.

"Pipe down, Maggie," he said, swinging her off his shoulder and into his arms. He was thigh deep in the water now, the cold stuff lapping against her suit-clad bottom. His eyes were dangerous. He had some point to make. "I want to hear you say that our age difference doesn't matter, or you're going down. Or in, depending on how you look at it."

She held on tightly to his neck. "But denying it's a problem isn't facing facts!"

"It's facing the wrong facts," he said. "The fact that we care about each other supersedes whatever minimal impact an eight-year difference could have on us."

"Dunk her, Dad!" Mike shouted. His friends cheered encouragement. "Dunk her! Dunk her!"

"If you dunk me," she said, nose to nose with him, "I am not letting go. If I go down—or in, so do you!"

"Well, the difference there," he said, holding her gaze, "is that you're afraid of a dunk in cold water and I'm not."

"No," she replied, "you're just afraid of being deprived of your apple fritter!"

"Ohhh," he said with a throaty warning and

tossed her away from him. She hadn't intended to let
go, but she was caught off guard and landed with a
chilling splash right on her pride and sank like a
stone.

She was plucked right out again, but found it hard
to berate a man who was kissing her. The boys
squealed and cheered and dunked each other.

Duffy finally brought everyone back to the sand,
handed her a towel and helped the boys dry off. Then
the boys went up the stairs onto the back deck to
play with the car and the plane.

"I'm going to get you for that," Maggie promised
darkly as he helped her dry her hair.

He kissed her earlobe. "I'm counting on that," he
said.

Chapter Nine

The four boys played just beyond the French doors all afternoon. Maggie and Duffy could do nothing but look at each other longingly and wait for nightfall.

Maggie tied her damp hair into a knot and busied herself making cookies while Duffy went to his workshop.

Maggie's London bank called to tell her that Eduard had been caught and her checking and savings accounts released. But her credit cards remained frozen until after his trial because the activity on them helped prove his whereabouts.

She thought a little sadly about the zealot and his cause. She might be able to sympathize with his cause but not his tactics.

Duffy's office in New York called in the middle of the afternoon. She took him the cordless phone.

"Hey, Pat," he said, turning off a small sanding tool he'd been working with. "Right. Luke's on Bobby Titus. He was going on his annual trek to

Ireland, as I recall." He listened a moment, then frowned. "What do you mean, missing?"

Maggie, about to leave the room, turned at the concerned sound of his voice.

He listened again. "Yeah, well sometimes people don't think they want to be protected as completely as we do. Where were they? Okay, look. Try the Full Tankard Pub. He gave me the slip once when I was in Dublin with him. He has a lady there. I know, just tell Luke to give it a try. If that doesn't work, call me."

He turned off the phone and got to his feet.

"A client got away?"

"Yeah." He pulled off a pair of protective glasses that hung around his neck and put them on a shelf. "He's a boxer, and he likes to go home once a year to visit the old place, but he's concerned for his safety and rightly so. He's a bit of a blowhard and talks disparagingly about everybody."

She was momentarily distracted by a detail. "Why would a boxer need a bodyguard?

"He might not be licensed to carry a weapon," he said, turning off power strips and lights. "He might be good in the ring, but not necessarily on the run or in a car or a multitude of other possibilities."

She nodded. "Then, why would he give a bodyguard the slip if he knows he needs protection?"

"Because of a woman."

"But, doesn't he want to arrive safely wherever she is?"

"I'm sure he does," he grinned. "But I don't

imagine he wants her to see that he has hired protection. I learned to be discreet about that, but Luke's new and thinks letting the world know your client's being protected wards off trouble.''

''Doesn't it?''

''Sometimes trouble just wants to be.''

And wasn't that profound, she thought, as he ushered her back into the kitchen. She'd forgotten the cookies and got a sniff of something burning.

''Rats!'' she cried, running toward the oven. The cookies were dark gold, the bottoms definitely burned.

''Not so bad,'' he said, looking over her shoulder. ''Mike likes them that way. I, however, am going to take one of these good ones.'' He reached to the countertop where several dozen were cooling on waxed paper.

He snapped one in half with a bite. ''Yum,'' he said when he'd swallowed. ''You used to bring these over when you sat with me all those years ago. They convinced me you'd make the perfect wife.''

She looked dispiritedly at the charred pan. ''That's because I never brought over the burned ones.'' He hooked an arm around her shoulders and drew her close. ''Can I have some detail on that nighttime entertainment you had planned?''

''If only to make you regretful,'' she said putting the pan aside and wrapping her arms around his waist. ''You dunked me, so I can only presume that means you didn't want it.''

"No," he corrected, kissing her forehead. "It means I want it, but I wanted to dunk you, too."

"Well, that's just selfish."

"Yeah. You may as well know the awful truth while you can still escape."

She leaned into him, thinking that there probably was no escape for her now. There were a lot of things to think about one day when there was time and she could think clearly. But that wasn't now. Particularly with his arms wrapped around her.

She sighed. "I hope your client's all right."

"I'm 99 percent sure he is," he replied.

She noticed that he sounded vaguely distracted and leaned out of his arms to look into his face.

"Something wrong?" she asked.

"No," he said, walking around her to go to the French windows. "I was just wondering where the boys are." He pushed the doors open and stepped outside. The car and plane stood there, the propeller turning slowly in the late-afternoon breeze.

He looked down, then leaned over the deck railing to look up the beach at the backs of the other homes. He stepped back inside. "Maybe they went upstairs and we didn't hear them in the shop."

Maggie felt the burgeoning of panic. She was always aware of the sound of the boys. At any point in time, long conditioning as a mother made it possible for her to pick out by the sounds where they were and what they were doing.

Until this afternoon when she'd been thinking about herself.

As Duffy ran upstairs, she went down the deck stairs and called their names. There was no answer. It was dinnertime, and there was not a sign of activity up or down the beach.

She turned at the sound of Duffy's footsteps on the deck stairs. He was looking worried.

"Could they have gone home with the twins?" she asked.

He nodded. "But they're not supposed to do that without asking. I'll go check." He pointed her upstairs. "Will you stay in case the office calls back?"

"Sure." She ran back up the steps, trying to stay calm. She'd seen them only...how many minutes ago? She'd taken cookies out to them, then come in and put another batch in. Shortly after that the office had called, she'd gone into the workroom to pass on the message, she and Duffy had talked. It couldn't have been more than ten minutes.

But anything could happen in ten minutes. One of them could have walked into the surf, or a stranger could have happened by, or— She stopped herself from thinking along those lines. There were four boys, not one alone. If one had wandered into the water, the other would have run back to report. If a stranger had happened by, he couldn't have taken all four of them without a major ruckus.

No. They'd simply gone to a neighbors or to town or something. Either they'd forgotten the rules in their excitement or had chosen to ignore them in favor of whatever they wanted to do. Her boys had sometimes been guilty of that.

Duffy was back in a few minutes, now looking really worried. Her own pulse began to speed.

"Not at the neighbors?" she asked, hating to.

He shook his head. "Neighbors aren't there. Judy just got back from town and hasn't seen them."

"Is there a playground in town?"

"No. Judy's going to walk the beach, and I'm going into the woods across the road. I'm taking the cell phone. If the office calls, tell them to call me on it." He pointed to the bulletin board in the kitchen. "They've got the number, but if you need it, it's on that yellow Post-it."

"Okay. Duffy, I'm sure they're fine, they just…you know how kids are." She wasn't really convinced of that, but she clung to the hope. Her own personal experience had taught her that loved ones could be overdue for very tragic reasons. But she didn't want that to happen to him.

"Just watch," she said bracingly. "They'll be here when you get back."

"Yeah," he said, giving her a quick hug, then snatching his jacket off the hook by the door and loping across the road and into the woods.

She went back inside, aware of the sudden, deafening silence. Her house in Devon had sounded like that the night she'd learned her husband and boys had died. It was as though the stillness resonated loneliness. Baldy had come to sit with her until her father arrived, but it hadn't helped. She'd felt lost in the silence, as though she'd died, too.

She pushed those memories away and busied herself putting the cookies in the Big Bird–shaped jar, made a fresh pot of coffee, washed the bowls and utensils she'd used and the cookie tins, then looked out the French doors to see the sky beginning to darken.

She began to pray, fighting to think positively. They were fine. They had to be fine. In the way of children caught up in the excitement of their games, they just forgot to come home. But where were they?

Safe, she told herself. They were safe. Just not…home.

The telephone rang and she jumped a foot, then swallowed and picked it up, praying for one of the boys' voices.

There was a moment's pause on the other end of the line when she said, "Hello?"

"Hello," a man's voice finally replied. "Is Duffy there, please? This is Patrick MacInnes from his office."

"He isn't here," she said, "but he asked me to tell you to call his cell phone if there's a further problem with Mr. Titus."

"Actually, there isn't," the man replied. "We found him where Duff said he might be." Another brief pause. "Is this Maggie?"

It was her turn to be surprised. "Yes."

"I'm glad you're back safe and sound," he said. He had a warm, confident voice. It reminded her of Duffy's. "I'm his friend as well as his business associate. I take care of things while he's gone." Then he asked in a careful tone, "Is everything all right there?"

"I'm not sure," she replied honestly. "He's out looking for the boys."

"*They're* missing?" he asked.

She sighed, uncertain how much of his personal business Duffy would want her to share. "Missing might be a little strong. They're just…late."

Another worried pause. "If you haven't found them in an hour, will you ask him to call me back? I can be there in a couple of hours."

"I will," she promised.

Nice, she thought, hanging up the phone, to have such devoted friends.

She became aware suddenly of the sound of a motor at the front of the house and went to investigate.

DUFFY HAD SHOUTED himself hoarse. The woods echoed with his shouts of "Mike! Adam!" Unfortunately there was no responding echo.

He'd beaten his way through the woods, all the way to the other side where a construction site had been clearing ground for a new home, hoping he'd find them there admiring the big equipment.

But he had no such luck. The site was closed down for the night, one emergency light left on to discourage theft or vandalism. He walked all around it, looked under and inside the equipment, praying for some sign of the boys, but there was nothing.

He stopped to shout again. Still nothing.

He went back into the woods and walked half a

mile south, then half a mile north, calling their names every few seconds, willing a response.

When it was finally too dark to see his hand in front of his face, he prepared to head home, a horrible, terrifying something in his gut he couldn't put a name to. It was anger and fear and an undefined emotion that dealt with what could happen to little boys taken by depraved strangers.

He wanted to fall to his knees, scream with the futility of searching and finding no sign, but he had to hold it together. He was trained to hold it together. But it was so much easier, he acknowledged guiltily, when it wasn't your own children.

And with sudden, paralyzing empathy, he had a clearer understanding of Maggie's grief. He hated himself for all the times he'd told her she had to put it behind her, move on, start over. What he felt was so big and ugly, there was no way to simply move past it. And he didn't even know yet what had happened to his—

The cell phone rang, interrupting his thoughts. He hoped selfishly that Ben had found Titus because he didn't think he could deal with that now.

He had just cleared the woods and stood on the road about a block north of his home. "Yes?" he demanded.

"Duffy, they're home." It was Maggie's jubilant voice. "They're fine. They went with the twins and their parents for ice cream. They thought…well, come on home and they'll explain."

He could have dissolved into a puddle of relief.

He even needed a moment before he could move. He stood still in the darkness dotted by front porch lights and thanked God for his mercy.

Then he started home. He was in a dangerous mood by the time he got there. His terror had been somewhat diminished, but the big ugly thing in his gut was readjusting itself to house another fear entirely. What was the point, he thought, in preaching safety rules to kids day in and day out when they simply forgot or ignored them when they chose?

He was going to have to do something about that.

He pushed the front door open and was proud of himself that it remained on its hinges. He marched through the living room, yanking off his jacket as he went, and stopped in the kitchen doorway to find his boys, pale and wide-eyed, seated at the table, Maggie standing protectively in front of it.

At first sight of their round and frightened little faces, he wanted to hug them to him for all eternity, so they'd never be endangered again. But he'd gone from the paralysis of relief to the restlessness of emotions too entangled to react to clearly. He didn't trust himself to touch them.

Maggie pulled a chair out for him. He ignored it.

"What happened?" he demanded.

"They…" Maggie began.

He silenced her with a look. "I'd like to hear it from them."

"Fine," she replied calmly.

He tried to intimidate her into silence again with

another look, but she went on calmly, "I just want to be sure you're listening."

He ignored her and turned to Mike. "Well?"

Mike looked terrified, and while Duffy hated that, he also hated what he'd felt only moments ago because of all the real dangers they might have faced.

"We went to see the new puppy Mr. Baker brought home," Mike said with a swallow. "It was just gonna take a minute, but we got playing with it, then Mrs. Baker asked us if we wanted to go with them for ice cream and to see how the puppy liked riding in the car. I tried to call and ask you, but the line was busy."

"Why didn't you just run back home and ask?"

"I…didn't think of it. I was gonna call you from the ice-cream place."

"And?"

"And…I forgot."

"I forgot, too," Adam chimed in. Duffy recognized that as an attempt to defend or at least support his brother, and while he appreciated that on one level, it only made him more angry on another.

"So all the times we've talked about the two of you not going anywhere unless you have my permission meant nothing?"

It *was* a loaded question. He didn't blame them for not answering.

"Did you tell Mrs. Baker that I said it was okay?"

"No," Mike said quickly. "She told me to call you on the phone, but she didn't know you didn't answer. She probably thought I talked to you."

"But *you* knew you didn't."

"I know," Mike agreed, desperate to get off the hook. "I was gonna call you from…"

"But you didn't!" Duffy shouted. He usually prided himself on never raising his voice, but at the moment he was beyond maintaining a reasonable standard. He pointed to the clock. "What time is it?" he demanded of Mike.

"Quarter of nine," Mike replied, his eyes brimming.

"What time did you go to the Bakers?"

Mike shrugged. "I don't know."

"I know!" Duffy shouted again. "I…"

"Duffy…" Maggie said quietly.

"Don't!" he said, pointing a finger at her. He turned his attention back to the boys. "I noticed you weren't on the deck at about five-thirty. How much time is that from then to now?"

It was no time for a math lesson, but he had a point to make.

Mike looked up at the clock and calculated. "Two hours and…"

"Three!" Duffy corrected. "Three hours and fifteen minutes we've been looking for you! I thought something awful had happened to you. I thought you'd drowned or were lost in the woods or kidnapped!"

"Duffy!" Maggie caught his arm and held when he tried to shake her off.

"Maggie…" he warned, certain he hadn't gotten through to them and knowing he had to.

"Duffy, you have to take a breath," she said reasonably.

"This," he said, patience strained to snapping, "is not your concern."

"Isn't it?" she asked, maintaining her hold on him. "Then, you're inviting me into your life just so far? I can be in the kitchen, in my bathing suit, in your arms, but not with your children?"

She had a point and he hated that. Now he was angry at them *and* at her. Fine. Then they could just deal with each other.

He grabbed his keys up off the table and looked from one boy to the other. "I'm too angry to deal with you right now. Get upstairs. Maggie's going to stay with you, and we'll talk when I get back." He turned to Maggie. "Remove your nails from my arm, please."

She seemed surprised to discover she still had hold of him. She freed him and said quietly, "I only want to help."

"Feel free," he said, heading for the door, "I'll be back."

MIKE AND ADAM BURST into tears as the sound of the Jeep's motor roared away. Maggie was tempted to join them but remembered that she had to be the adult.

"Okay, you heard your dad," she said. "Go upstairs and get ready for bed." She took each boy by the hand and led a sorry, tearful parade up the stairs.

She put Adam in the bathtub, then adjusted the

shower for Mike. She shampooed hair, helped them dry off and found clean pajamas.

"Did you have anything for dinner," she asked, "or just ice cream?"

"Just ice cream," Mike replied.

"I'm hungry!" Adam complained.

Maggie had never thought it reasonable to use bed without supper as punishment. She shooed them off to their rooms. "Be very quiet and I'll bring you something to eat."

She carried sandwiches and milk upstairs, and as she delivered Mike's, she looked up to see Adam in the doorway looking uncertain and pathetic.

"Can I eat in here, too?" he asked.

There was plenty of room in the double bed, but she looked at Mike for an answer. "Yeah," he said.

Adam climbed under the covers and asked worriedly as she distributed sandwiches. "Is Daddy gonna come back?"

Before Maggie could assure them that he would, Mike answered, "Of course he will. He's our dad."

"But he was real mad."

"I've known him longer than you. He'll come back."

"He doesn't love us anymore."

Again Maggie opened her mouth, but Mike answered first, "Yes, he does. When we're bad, he doesn't like what we do but he always loves us."

"But he was yelling."

"That's love," Mike said. "Sometimes it's... loud."

Maggie suddenly felt better about everything. She'd been afraid Duffy was about to lose control, but Mike's experience with his father seemed to have helped him get the message very clearly that they were loved unconditionally, and that Duffy's anger had been justified.

"He was angry," Maggie explained to Adam as he took a bite of his sandwich, "because we were very, very worried about you. He thought something terrible had happened because you knew the rules and he was sure you'd obey them. So when you weren't there, and you hadn't called to tell us where you were, all we could think was that something bad had happened."

Mike nodded. "I'm sorry. We were playing and I forgot."

"You should never have gone in the first place," she put in, seizing the opportunity, "without getting permission first."

"I know."

"You should see how cute the puppy is!" Adam, reassured that his father was coming back and recovering from the confrontation trauma, was almost his old self again. He munched heartily on his sandwich. "And at the ice-cream place, there's this room in the back with slides and stuff to climb over!"

Mike frowned at him. "Don't talk about it. We weren't supposed to be there."

"You think we could have a puppy?"

"I wouldn't ask for it right now," Maggie advised. "Now eat your sandwiches, drink your milk and call me when you're ready to be tucked in."

"Are you gonna stay?" Mike asked, his sandwich half-gone. He took a deep gulp of milk. "I mean—you know—all the time?"

She tried to evade a straight answer. "I live in London, Mike."

He nodded. "And we live in New York sometimes. But we move around. You could move around."

"Yes, I could." It seemed safe enough to agree to that.

"Your little boys died, didn't they?" he asked with youthful candor.

She didn't feel the panic that fact used to inspire. Pain pinched and ached but allowed her to accept the truth for what it was—a part of her life that was over. "Yes, they did," she answered. "You remind me a lot of them."

He seemed to like that idea. "How come?"

"Because they were full of fun, too. And I was always happy when I was with them."

Adam beamed and said to Mike, "We make her happy."

"You finish up," she said, taking the tray, "and call when you're ready for tucking in."

"Can we have dessert?" Adam asked.

She never withheld dinner, but she had been known to deny dessert. "No. Dessert's a treat, and you don't have one coming tonight."

Adam sighed. "I smelled cookies."

Maggie had cleaned up downstairs and was just beginning to worry about Duffy when the boys called her. Adam had gone back to his bed, and she hugged him firmly and tucked him in.

"If we had a puppy," he said, "it could sleep on my bed. Mike would feed it 'cause I'd probably forget. We could name it Blackie."

She stroked his unruly hair out of his eyes. "What if it was yellow?"

"Then we'd call it..." He thought about that. "Yellowie sounds stupid."

It was growing difficult to maintain her stern demeanor. "Maybe Goldie or Daisy or Buttercup."

He made a face. "Those aren't boy's names."

"Brandy?"

"That's a girl's name, too. I think we better get a black one." He smiled broadly. "I love you, Maggie," he said, then snuggled into his pillow.

A little shaken, she walked into Mike's room. He was staring at the ceiling. "I wish I'd remembered to call," he said. "I wish I hadn't made Dad worry."

"The best way to show you're sorry," she said, tucking the blankets in around his feet, "is to do your best not to do that again."

"Yeah."

She hugged him, then tucked the blankets in around his shoulders.

"What kind of cookies did you make?" he asked.

"Peanut butter," she replied, "with chocolate chips."

"Maybe we can have some tomorrow."

"Maybe."

"It'd be good if you could stay with us," he said as she turned off the light. "And not just because of the cookies."

She kissed his forehead and left the room, letting his door stand halfway open.

She poured herself a cup of coffee and waited for Duffy in the living room. She wondered if she'd damaged the tenuous hold they'd gotten on a relationship by interceding for his boys. As warm and welcoming as he'd been to her since he'd brought her home, it was clear that he'd resented her interference.

Perhaps that was just the heat of the moment and he'd since thought twice about it.

But if that was the case, where was he?

She tried to imagine going back to London and couldn't. The picture simply wouldn't form. Despite all her efforts to hold herself apart, she'd clicked into place here.

Still, that might not mean anything if Duffy decided he didn't want to share his life after all.

She pushed the French doors open and stepped out onto the deck. The night was clear and balmy, and the breeze carried the rich fragrance of the sea and the trees.

She drew in a deep breath and prayed that Duffy was safe and thinking about her.

Chapter Ten

Duffy was calm again as he pulled into the driveway of his home. It had taken a two-hour walk on the beach to settle him down to the place where he could remember that Mike and Adam were just children and would probably terrify him again and in more awful ways before they were grown. And to understand that Maggie's defense of them had been a maternal reaction, and a really good thing if he was hoping they'd one day be a family. He just wasn't used to having his judgment questioned. He would have to work on that.

The house was dark when he walked in, and he was afraid for a minute that Maggie had gone to bed. Then he saw that the French doors were open, and he caught a glimpse of her hair in the moonlight.

She turned at the sound of his footsteps and walked into the living room, pulling the doors closed behind her. She looked wary. Probably afraid, he thought, of the man who'd shouted at his children, then told her to butt out—or close enough.

Every system in his body accelerated at the sight

of her. Everything he wanted to say seemed to recede from him as feelings took over. All the banked energy from that evening, all the words he hadn't shouted, all the things he hadn't broken still demanded satisfaction. He fought it, unwilling to lose his cool with her a second time.

He stopped several feet from her and said softly, "I'm sorry. You were right. I had to stop and think. I..."

To his utter and complete surprise, she walked into his arms. "I know how you felt. I was terrified, too. But they really are sorry. Mike's particularly upset. I know that doesn't diminish the worry, but it's nice to know your child has a conscience and an appreciation of your feelings, even if he didn't stop to think about those things before scaring the wits out of you."

There was something very liberating about hearing her commiserate with him. His fear had been such an isolating thing, particularly because he was used to being solely and completely responsible for his boys. And therefore alone in his misery when they disobeyed or disappointed him.

She tipped her head back to look into his eyes, her own expression stubborn. "I was trying to help," she said, "not interfere."

"I know," he said, drawing her back to him, holding her close. "I know. I apologize all over the place. And I'm grateful you were here to stay with them while I recovered my composure."

"I was happy to," she said. "I love them to pieces."

"Are they asleep?"

"I just checked. Adam is, but Mike might still be up."

"I'm going to run upstairs for a minute," he said, drawing her arms from around him. "You want to pour a couple of glasses of wine?"

She reached up to plant a quick kiss on his lips. "I don't need the wine. I'll be waiting on the deck."

His heart kicked him like a mule. Everything inside him ticked and clamored. For an instant, he was sure he'd misunderstood, then he looked deeply into her eyes, into her promising smile, and knew he'd have understood that look even if he'd been dead.

Fortunately, his paternal instincts were so strong they fought their way through his libido and his raging anticipation to help him deal with his son.

Mike was sitting up in bed when he walked into his room. He even reached over to turn on his Scooby-Doo bedside lamp.

"Hi," Mike whispered.

Duffy sat on the edge of his bed and wrapped him in a hug. "Hi," he returned. "I'm glad you're still up. I wanted to talk to you about tonight."

Mike nodded seriously. "I'm sorry, Dad. I know that was wrong, but mostly it was because I knew what I was supposed to do but I kept forgetting."

"Some things are too important to your own safety for you to forget them. The rules aren't just to annoy you, they're because I know all the things that can hurt you, and you don't. So you have to trust that I know what I'm doing.''

"I do." Mike nodded. ''Adam was afraid you weren't coming back.''

"What?'' That horrified him on a new level.

Mike shook his head and grinned. ''He's never seen you that mad. And he doesn't know you like I know you. I told him you'd be back. And Maggie explained why you were so mad—'cause you thought something awful had happened to us.''

"That's right,'' he said, his distress diminishing just a little at Mike's confidence in him. ''And you scared Maggie, too. You guys are grounded for a week to make sure you don't forget again.''

Mike took that with equanimity. Then he asked gravely, ''Is Maggie gonna stay?''

"We haven't talked about that yet,'' he replied, though he knew they had to.

Mike leaned forward, his eyes bright with something to share. Duffy leaned in to listen.

"I asked her if she was gonna stay, and she said she lives in London.''

That was a depressing answer. ''She does,'' he had to confirm.

"But I said she could move around like we do, from New York to Maine, and she said maybe she could.''

"She did?''

"Yeah, and you know what else?''

"What?''

Mike beamed. "She said me and Adam remind her of her little boys."

"Really."

"Yes, 'cause they were fun to be with and she's happy when she's with us."

Now, that was hopeful. "Wow."

"But she said we shouldn't ask for a puppy."

"A puppy?" This was becoming an intricate conversation.

"Yeah. Adam wanted to know if you'd get us a puppy. Jake and Jamie's is so cute!"

A puppy. He didn't think his mind could deal with that right now. "A puppy's an awful lot of work. And when I'm at work and you're at school, it'd spend a lot of time alone."

"Desiree would be home."

"Yes, but it wouldn't be fair to make her responsible for it when we're not around."

"If Maggie stays, she'd be around. A lot of moms stay home and do stuff in the house. You know. Cook and make stuff. Sometimes they drive around."

"Maggie's an actress," he reminded him. Although, Duffy's mind played back the thoughts she'd shared about summer stock if she lived in Lamplight Harbor. "Even if she did decide to stay with us, she might be gone a lot, too."

Mike grinned. "Maybe we could get one of those people who can teach us at home so me and Adam can stay with the puppy."

Duffy had to appreciate his resourcefulness. "You

mean a tutor," he said, pushing him gently back to the pillow and pulling up his covers. "Let's talk about this tomorrow. There's a lot to think about."

Mike snuggled down and reached his arms up for a hug. "But, that's not a no, right?"

"It's not a no," he agreed, wrapping him close.

"Okay. 'Night, Dad."

"Good night, Mike. I love you."

"I love you, too."

Duffy looked into Adam's room and found him fast asleep as Maggie had said he was. One bare foot stuck out of the blankets as usual, and Duffy went in to cover the foot and touch the curly blond head. It was hard to believe that the beautiful little angel face had been partially responsible for the agonies of earlier tonight.

Duffy pulled Adam's door partially closed, then stopped at the top of the stairs before going down.

Now he had to deal with Maggie. Shifting gears from father to lover should allow more time for preparation. But now that he knew the boys were safe, his own situation required his attention.

He wanted to race down the stairs, but he took them slowly, forcing himself to think, to take the time. After all—what if he'd read more into her simple, "I'll be waiting for you on the deck," than she'd intended?

MAGGIE WAS HALFWAY across the living room, going toward the kitchen, when she heard Duffy on the stairs. She was going to pour that wine after all, her confidence of a few moments ago disintegrating the longer she waited for Duffy to return.

What if he wasn't as eager for her as she was for him? she wondered. True, he'd implied that often enough, even said it clearly a time or two, but she'd put him off, called him crazy, denied that she felt anything in return. It was entirely possible that her revelation had come too late.

And he was moving lazily on the stairs as though he had all the time in the world. She watched his long, lean legs in the faded jeans, the easy line of his shoulders in his short-sleeved white sweatshirt stained and pulled from his search through the woods, and yearned for him with a depth of longing she'd once been so sure she'd never experience again.

He wasn't, *couldn't* be feeling the same desire tormenting her.

He stopped two steps from the bottom, his gaze catching and holding hers as though questioning something he'd seen in it.

Suddenly embarrassed by her eagerness, when she was older than he and should be…should be… She didn't know what she should be or how she should feel. It was all too powerful to stand still for analysis.

She pointed to the kitchen. ''I was going…to get that wine. I'm…ah…''

As he came down the last two steps and toward her, she wanted to run past him into the kitchen, but he was too close. And she didn't think she could move, anyway.

He took her face in his hands, and his eyes seemed to devour her, feature by feature.

"There's love *and* fear in your eyes," he said, a pleat of concern between his. "Love isn't supposed to make you afraid."

She felt herself melt at his touch, at the warm, soothing sound of his voice. All worldly wisdom seemed to abandon her, and she stood vulnerable and anxious as one of his hands smoothed back her hair.

"That isn't fear," she admitted, her voice barely there. "It's…worry, I guess."

"Why?"

"Because…" Honesty, she realized, was the only thing that was going to get them through this. And she knew him well enough now—or again—to know that he'd tell her the truth. So, she drew a breath and plunged in. "Because I finally understand how I feel about you, but I understand that you might have changed your mind in the interim, or at least had second—ah!"

She uttered a shocked little scream when he swept her up into his arms. He carried her to the sofa and placed her on it, sitting beside her and loosening his grip just long enough to look into her face. He was smiling, though desire smoked in his eyes.

"You thought," he asked in disbelief, "that I could change my mind about loving you?"

His amusement at that notion was flattering, but she felt obligated to make him think about it.

"Making love with you," she whispered, her arms still looped around his neck, "is a monumental step for me. If I'm more…eager for this than you are, I wish you'd be hon—ah!''

In another move that surprised her, he reached under her shirt and pushed it up and over her head. When she emerged from the neckline, her hair tumbled around her face, Duffy kissed her senseless.

''It's monumental for me, too,'' he said seriously, ''because I've loved you forever.'' Then he smiled and kissed her again as he reached around to unfasten her bra. ''But you have to stop gasping. You'll wake the boys.''

How was she to stop gasping, she wondered, when his hands were everywhere, pulling her shoes and socks off, skimming her shorts and panties down her legs, tracing the line of her limbs up to her waist as his eyes watched their progress with a fascination that bordered on reverence? Her whole body was gasping.

She'd forgotten what it was like to have her skin come alive under a lover's touch, to have the controlled person she knew herself to be transformed into a sexual being aquiver with anticipation, control happily surrendered to whatever awaited.

She reached with fumbling fingers for the hem of his sweatshirt. He helped her pull it off, then kissed her deeply as she reached under his T-shirt and connected with warm, muscled flesh.

He groaned and drew her closer to him, hands splayed against her back. She felt the rough denim of his jeans against her bare legs as she placed a knee between his for the leverage to pull off his undershirt.

He took advantage of the opportunity to take her breast into his mouth. She gasped again, then slapped a hand over her mouth as they stopped still, expecting discovery. But everything remained quiet.

He tipped her onto her back on the cushions and stood to remove his tennis shoes and socks, then peel off his jeans and briefs.

He was magnificent, and his security in his nakedness made her suddenly a little nervous about her own.

He saw the change in her expression instantly. She sat up guiltily, knowing she'd upset a momentum men were usually very sensitive about.

He sat beside her and asked with gentle patience, "What? Am I now more eager to do this than you are?"

"I doubt that," she said with sincerity.

"Then, what is it?"

She put her hands to his shoulders. Her touch against his bare skin made him feel as though she'd lit a match to his insides. His patience struggled against his control.

"I was just thinking how strong and magnificent you look," she said, again with a sincerity that humbled him.

He couldn't find the problem in that. "Why does that upset you?"

She held both hands up helplessly. "Even regular workouts can't fight the effects of age and gravity. And I'm not as religious about my diet as—ah!"

He pushed her back to the pillows and pinned her

there with a finger across her lips. "We're through with discussions of age," he said firmly, "gravity, and whatever the hell else you can think of to put in our way. I *adore* you, so can we just focus on making love to each other? Please?"

"Well, you asked me." He offered his hand and she took it. He pulled her to her feet.

"Because I thought you might have a *real* concern." He took her place on the sofa and drew her down atop him.

"The state of my body might be a real concern to you," she argued.

"It's going to be a real concern to you," he threatened, "if you don't stop it. Now, be quiet and do something to redeem yourself."

She did. She was clever and graceful and clearly as eager as she'd admitted. He had to wrest control away from her. He caught her hands in one of his and held them still while she sat astride his waist and looked at him in surprise.

"You want me to stop?" she asked.

"No," he replied breathlessly, "but I'd like you a little more involved."

He was sure she knew what he meant, but she pretended to misunderstand. She grinned wickedly. "If I was any more involved, we'd be…"

He pulled her upper body gently down to his chest and stroked a hand over her hip to the back of her thigh. "You can take some pleasure in this, too, Maggie," he said softly, as his hand traced her graceful lines. "I know this is the first time in a long time, but you can participate. It's all right. I'm not Harry, but it's all right.''

She pushed against his chest to look down at him, her expression stricken. He was afraid for one horrible moment that he'd said something irretrievable.

But she seemed to be afraid that he was the one who'd been hurt. ''I know you're not Harry. I loved him desperately. But I love *you* desperately, and I'd never be in danger of mixing you up.''

''Then, why?'' he asked, stroking up and down her thigh, ''are you determined to do all the giving and none of the taking? Are you thinking you won't be betraying Harry if you don't actually take pleasure from it?''

She seemed to be thinking that through, her blue eyes liquid in the shadows. ''I don't think so. At least not…consciously. Am I?'' A tear fell and she sank onto him again. ''Am I doing that and just don't know it because he was my first and I've never… Oh, no. I'm not going to mess this up, am I?''

''I don't think that's possible,'' he said, holding her to him with one hand, while his other hand explored that tantalizing curve of her hip. ''Just think less and feel more while I take over, okay?''

''Okay.''

She wanted this to be right for him. Because there was no way it couldn't be right for her. He'd rescued her, cared for her, amused her and even in a few ways, educated her. He'd captured her heart, given her hope and shared his children with her.

Secretly, the thought had crossed her mind that her

enthusiasm in making love with him might make up for whatever she lacked in style or inventiveness. Harry had been her only experience, and though they'd had a wonderful time together, he'd been a little staid in his approach and had appreciated the same level of attention in the bedroom that she gave him in every other phase of their lives.

He had always pleased her, but he'd never taken his time about it. This was something new for her.

While her body quivered with Duffy's attentive explorations, the monitoring part of her brain was listing sensations. There were some she remembered, though it had been a long time, and some that were completely new and startling in their ability to paralyze her with their power.

Duffy touched inside her and she heard her own little sound of pleasure. He stifled it with a kiss and stilled her with tiny, subtle strokes that pinned her to him in a tortured waiting.

She gasped again as pleasure approached like a promise.

Duffy shifted her so that she was poised over him, then entered her with an easy sway of hip. She held to him a little nervously. "I've never…been on top!" she gasped in a whisper

He linked his fingers in hers to lend her balance. "Relax," he advised quietly, "and follow me."

He moved gently under her and she found it easy to sway in concert. It made her feel elemental, like a flower nourished by the earth.

And as pleasure came upon her in a rush, overriding all old pain to fill every dark little corner of her body with light, she felt herself blossom.

Duffy shuddered with his own pleasure while still very much aware of hers. For a moment, there, he'd been afraid she'd be unwilling to give her heart to their endeavor. But she had. It had been in every touch of her fingers, in the way she'd leaned into him and let him lead the way.

She finally collapsed on him, her eyes bright and brimming with tears in the shadows as she folded her hands on his chest and rested her chin on them. "I...don't know what to say," she whispered.

He pulled the cotton throw off the back of the sofa and spread it over her, anchoring it with his arms. "Do you have to say anything?"

"I'm used to having brilliant things to say after an emotional event," she said, putting the tip of an index finger to his chin. "To turning to the audience with an insightful wrap-up of the action, and a pouring out of all I feel about it. But..." She shook her head as though that would be impossible. "I can't do that."

He felt a moment's trepidation. "Because you don't know what you feel?"

She blinked. "No. Because there are no words."

He accepted that with the grace the humbling words deserved.

"Will you marry me, Maggie?" he asked.

"Yes, Duffy," she replied simply.

He thought it fortunate that the confines of the couch required that he be on the bottom. Otherwise he'd have fallen off in surprise.

Chapter Eleven

Duffy didn't want Maggie to know that her easy affirmative had shocked him. He behaved as though it was precisely what he'd expected.

"The boys will be very happy," he said, catching her fingertips and kissing them.

"So will I," she replied, bringing his hand back to her lips.

"As soon as your father comes back." He fought down a shout of triumph and tried to keep talking as though he'd thought all this through, confident in her agreement.

"Okay."

"Here or in London?"

"Oh, here," she said with a sigh, resting her cheek on his chest. "In that little white church with the steeple as you come into town."

"Where do you want to live?"

"Here," she said again, then lifted her face to smile into his. "Or do we have to stay in New York until you're really ready to do something else?"

His heart was going to burst right through his

chest. That answer changed everything. "No, we don't. I was going to take Patrick in as a partner. I can just let him buy me out instead. I'm sure he'd jump at the chance."

"Is he in a position to do that?"

"I think so, but if he isn't, I can make it easy for him. But, Maggie. Do you really want to give up the stage? I'd never ask that of you."

She sighed and traced the line of his clavicle with her fingernail. "I haven't missed it," she said, apparently a little surprised by that fact. "I expected to, but I haven't. So much has changed since I've been here. *I've* changed since I've been here. I suppose if I discover that I miss acting, I can start that summer stock company I was imagining the other day."

"We'll keep Desiree on," he said, "so that you can do whatever you want with your day. Or we can send for Eponine."

His mind was boggled by the thought of her as the mother of his children, and himself with a little furniture shop downtown, working on her theatrical productions in the summer.

"God, Duffy," she said on a whisper. "Is this really happening to us?"

He held her closely. "Yes. It's really happening."

Maggie basked in his loving and protective embrace. She was free to be herself again, not the woman who'd felt so lost in the world she'd had to be other characters in order to know what to say and think and feel. It was safe to be Maggie again because Duffy loved her and understood.

She smiled to herself at the thought of mothering his boys. She was going to love that. The future stretched out ahead of her like a sun-dappled road. Nothing was ever perfect, but love gave life meaning, and she was eager to devote herself to it again.

She stifled a yawn and rested her cheek against Duffy's chest again.

"Go to sleep," he said, stroking her hair. "There's lots of time to iron out details."

"The boys," she said sleepily, "want a puppy."

"So Mike told me. How do you feel about that?"

"I love dogs. We were just never home enough."

"We have time to work that out, too."

She kissed the tight indentation between his pectoral muscles. "Good night, Duffy."

He kissed her forehead. "Good night."

MAGGIE AWOKE to a loud banging. She heard the children's voices, a man's shouts and a voice she thought she recognized from last night's phone conversation, raised in annoyance. And something was being forced over her head. She was completely disoriented for a moment, until Duffy's face appeared as he yanked his sweatshirt down to her waist.

"If you keep the blanket over your bottom half," he whispered with a grin. "No one will ever know what we've been up to." He had pulled on his jeans and T-shirt.

"What is it?" she asked groggily.

He kissed her lightly. "Reinforcements, I think."
And he went to the door where Mike was leaping up
to try to unfasten the latch just beyond his fingertips.

"It's Uncle Patrick!" Adam exclaimed, peering
through the drapes. "And he's yelling at Judy!"

Duffy lifted Mike aside, unlatched the door and
opened it. Maggie remembered with horror that she'd
promised to call Patrick when the boys were found,
and she'd forgotten.

"I'm Pat MacInnes!" he was saying loudly.
"I…"

"I don't care who you are!" Judy was saying, her
color high, her long, black braid swinging with em-
phasis as she pointed at Pat. "I'm telling you they
had a very trying night and you have no business
pounding…"

"I'll pound if I want to!" he roared back at her.
"I'm a friend of the family and I want to know—"
He stopped abruptly at the sight of Duffy and the
boys in the doorway. The thunder left his expression
as he smiled widely and scooped up a pajama-clad
boy in each arm. They laughed delightedly.

"Well, here you are!" he said, settling each on a
muscular forearm. "Are you okay? No cuts and
bruises? No broken bones?" He looked to Duffy for
an answer.

"They're fine," Duffy replied, opening the door
wider. "Come on in."

Judy, looking a little disgruntled, wrapped a loud
plaid cotton robe around herself and started to head
back to her place.

"Judy!" he shouted. "Join us for coffee."

She shook her head. "Thanks, but I've got lots to do this morning. I was just trying to protect you from intrusion at this *ungodly hour*." She added the last two words in a loud voice aimed directly at Patrick's back.

He swung around, still holding the boys. "If you'd listened to me, Miss Buttinsky," he said, emphasizing the title he'd bestowed, "you'd have heard me say I was a friend of the family. But you were too busy flinging accusations of—"

"Whoa!" Duffy said, looking from one to the other in confusion. He pointed Patrick inside, then reached out to catch Judy's arm and physically pull her over the doorstep. "I'm making a pot of coffee, and you're going to watch the boys for me while I run to town and buy doughnuts and Maggie puts some clothes on."

Maggie looked at Duffy in mortification. So much for his theory that if she remained seated under the blanket, no one would know what they'd been up to.

Duffy grinned apologetically. "Maggie, this is my friend and business associate, Patrick MacInnes. Pat, Maggie Lawton."

Pat nodded affably. "We spoke on the phone last night." He added with a teasing frown. "You were supposed to call me back."

She nodded apologetically. "I'm so sorry. I forgot."

Duffy pointed them to the kitchen. "Make yourself comfortable. I won't be fifteen minutes. And try to be civilized, for heaven's sake.''

Maggie took advantage of their turned backs and ran upstairs as Duffy headed out the door to the bakery.

Half an hour later, over raspberry croissants, Duffy made a verbal agreement to sell his security firm to Patrick, who was surprised but more than willing to buy. He seemed pleased about the wedding, though astonished by the swiftness with which Duffy was changing his life.

The boys were happy with the news.

''You mean we're going to have a mom?'' Mike demanded as Duffy explained why he was selling the business and why Mike would be starting school in Lamplight Harbor. ''And live here all the time?''

Duffy nodded. ''Yes. Is that alright with you guys?''

Maggie waited nervously for their answer.

''Our own mom?'' Adam's eyes widened. ''And she'd call us 'honey' and 'sweetheart' and stuff like that?''

Duffy grinned at Maggie, asking her to answer that one.

''Yes, sweetheart,'' she replied. ''I'm going to be your own mom.''

Mike came closer, apparently needing details. ''You'll pick us up from school, and make soup, and comb our hair?''

''Yes,'' Maggie confirmed.

Mike grinned broadly but Adam looked concerned.

"You don't like the idea?" she asked, her heart sinking.

He leaned into her with a frown. "You're not going to make us eat eggplant, are you?"

"No," she assured him quickly. "I hate eggplant."

Both boys wrapped their arms around her.

While the men ironed out the details of the purchase, Judy volunteered to provide flowers for the wedding.

The boys, excited by the news that Maggie was staying, had gone out onto the deck to play with the car and the plane.

"You're sure you're not upset?" Maggie asked Judy quietly as the men went over figures at the other end of the table.

Judy looked confused for a moment, then seemed to understand. "No, no. My interest in Duffy has been as a neighbor and a friend, nothing more. Men are very entertaining, but I do *not* want my own."

"Why not?"

"They're just too much trouble. And I prefer my own company."

Maggie smiled, remembering that she'd felt that way a few short weeks ago.

Patrick left for New York right after lunch with the promise to return to serve as best man at the wedding. He hugged the boys, then Maggie, then bowed formally to Judy.

"Miss Buttinsky," he said, opening the door.

"Mr. Know-It-All," she replied.

He stepped into a cab, ignoring her.

Duffy grinned as Judy shuffled back to her place.

"That was interesting," he said to Maggie. "I've never known either of them to get that upset about anything."

"They were both worried about the boys."

"Yeah," he said. "That must have been it."

The sound of the ringing telephone sent them back into the house.

It was Maggie's father.

"Hi!" he said, sounding cheerful. "I've almost got this wrapped up," he said. "How's it going there?"

"It's going well," she replied, unwilling to tell him her good news over the phone. "So, when will you be home?"

"Very soon," he assured her.

"A few days? A week?"

"Depends on how long it takes us to write it up. We've verbally agreed on terms. We just have to prepare a deal they're willing to sign. You know what they say. God is in the details. Or some say the devil is in the details. Depends, I guess, on whether you love or hate what you're doing."

"Just hurry home, okay?"

"Okay."

DUFFY FOUND HIMSELF wishing the wedding was already a done deal. He'd always considered himself a man of faith—both in God and in his fellow man. But he was worried about this. He'd wanted Maggie Lawton most of his life, and now that she was about to become a part of it, he was suffering an odd sense of unreality.

''This can't happen to *you!*'' some little demon deep within kept telling him. 'Who do you think you are to believe you can step into this woman's life and be what she needs at a point when she's been so lost and alone?'

He told himself to shut up, that he might not deserve her but she'd decided she needed him as much as he needed her, and they were going to join forces. The children loved her and she loved them, and a relationship based on mutual need was a good, strong connection—whether or not he was worthy.

The voice, obviously intimidated by his superior powers of argument, was quiet for three whole days. Duffy felt confident as he and Maggie and the boys looked at school clothes in town, choosing to wait until the last minute to buy them because of the rate at which the boys were growing.

They sunbathed, played volleyball on the beach and ate breakfast and lunch on the deck. They had dinner by candlelight at the table, which the boys found exciting.

On the fourth night, desperate for some time alone with Maggie, Duffy asked Judy if she would watch the boys so he could take Maggie to Owl's Head for dinner.

She agreed, and the boys, at first disappointed at

being left out, were excited when Judy announced she planned to rent a Disney movie and order pizza.

Maggie went to town that afternoon, supposedly to buy stockings, and returned with her hair cut just below her ears. Duffy studied the short, curly do and put a hand to his heart where a pain had formed. A groan of disappointment tried desperately to erupt.

"You look cool!" Mike said enthusiastically.

"You look beautiful!" Adam tried to do him one better.

Duffy was afraid to speak, for fear the groan would come out despite his efforts to withhold it.

Maggie frowned. "You don't like it," she guessed, and went to the hall mirror to fluff the short, curly sides with her hand. "I thought it was...you know. Less theatrical and more serious."

"Uh...it looks very nice," he forced himself to say. It did look nice, he just had ripe memories of its former silky length spread over his face, running along his body with her kisses.

"Well, that was unconvincing." She looked in the mirror again. "You don't think it makes me look more suburban motherish?"

He made himself look at what the short hair did to the contour of her face.

It did emphasize the pleasing shape of her small chin and her wide, bright eyes. As he studied her, she tipped her head and teasingly struck a hollow-cheeked pose.

He laughed. The long hair had lent her drama; the

short style made her seem perky and had a surprisingly flirtatious quality all its own.

He kissed her, finally conceding that he liked it.

"It's a good thing," she told him, returning his kiss, "because you're going to have to live with it a good long time before it grows back. If I let it. I'm getting a little old for…"

She stopped at his warning look.

"Too old for long hair," she put in quickly. "Not for you."

"All right, then," he said, pushing her toward the stairs. "I made reservations. We should leave in forty-five minutes if we're going to make it in time."

He was showered, changed and putting on a cotton jacket over an open-necked white shirt when she walked out of the bathroom in a round-necked black lace dress that skimmed her knees. The breath left him as though someone had opened a door in space. She might decide to leave the stage, he thought, but the presence she'd acquired by years of walking upon it would never leave her. She was the essence of woman in its most perfect form—grace, intelligence and beauty all contained in a shapely package.

"You look gorgeous," he said reverently.

She came to wrap her arms around his neck and kiss him, whispering, "So do you."

Her fragrant embrace was sincere, and her eyes were filled with love. As he wrapped an arm around her and led her down the stairs, he couldn't imagine what he'd been worried about.

The restaurant was in the bottom floor of a hotel

ten miles away. It was built on a bluff overlooking the ocean and decorated in the style of Caribbean opulence. The lobby was filled with palm trees, small, glass-topped tables and rattan furniture.

In the restaurant they were seated in cathedral-back chairs at a table covered in white linen and set with gold-rimmed china, crystal and silver. In the middle of the table were red roses in a silver bowl. A single silver candlestick stood beside it.

Maggie put a fingertip to a rose petal. "Don't you love the civilizing influence of fine things? I love the beach just as I loved our farm in Devon, but sometimes you need the reminder of the elegance to which we can rise when given the opportunity. Silly, I know, but maybe it raises something inside, too."

"I'm sure it does," he replied. "You can see it in the kids. They quiet down instantly when we walk into an elegant place. As though they know instinctively that the surroundings require different behavior."

"You've done such a good job with them." She leaned back as the waiter brought menus. "I'm sure I don't have to tell you how remarkable you are to have taken responsibility for Mike."

He shrugged off her praise. "Adam was mine, and Mike always felt like mine. It was an easy decision." He reminded her with a glance over the top of his menu, "You're doing the same thing."

"A much easier decision with one parent already in place." She perused the menu. "What do you recommend?"

They discussed the merits of satisfying steaks over the exotic spices in a prawn dish. They finally decided to try both and share.

"I think that means we fail in the rising-to-the-elegance-of-our-surroundings phenomenon," she said, toasting him with her wine. "Sharing off your plate is the kind of thing you do at picnics."

He touched his glass to hers. "We'll be discreet. I wouldn't know what to do if there wasn't a kid picking off my plate, or if I wasn't having to finish off somebody's veg—What?"

Maggie's eyes had been skimming their surroundings as he talked, and they suddenly widened in stunned surprise as she focused on something behind him. She sloshed the wine in her glass as she put it down on the table and stood.

"Maggie!" he said as she put her napkin on the table and ran off toward the lobby.

He followed, excusing himself to the waiter who was bringing rolls and butter.

He stopped in the doorway where she'd stopped and saw what had caught her attention. Seated at a small table visible from the dining room were two nicely dressed older gentlemen talking and laughing over their port. They were Maggie's father and his own!

Maggie marched toward the table and he followed in her wake, unsure what to make of what he saw...until the two men looked up as she approached the table. Guilt as well as shock was clearly visible in both pairs of eyes.

"What are you doing here?" she demanded of her father, who leaned back in his chair as she stood over him. "I thought you were out of the country. You told me you'd call when you were coming home. How long have you *been* home? And how's your *heart,* Dad?"

Mike looked at Charlie. Charlie's glance bounced off Duffy, then Maggie, before returning to Elliott with a trapped look.

"When did you come back?" Maggie demanded. "When?" Then as Elliott stuttered and stammered and Charlie sank deeper into his chair, she said in a low, frightful voice, "Nooo."

"Maggie, I…" Elliott tried to explain.

Maggie had both hands on her hips and wore an expression Duffy was happy he didn't have to face. "You never left, did you?" she asked, her voice rising.

Duffy came up behind her to put an arm around her in an attempt to encourage her to calm down. He suddenly realized what had happened, too.

He remembered his father's curious behavior when he brought Maggie home, then his urgency to leave the following morning when he usually liked to visit for several days. He'd apparently been anxious to rejoin Elliott and leave him and Maggie to let nature take its course.

Duffy was more amused than upset. But then, he hadn't been kidnapped, whisked across the ocean on a plea to visit her father, then been told he'd been sent away on State Department business and been forced to stay elsewhere.

She lowered her voice, but he could feel her fury under his hands. "I don't understand! I came all this way to see you, and you…"

"They were in collusion," Duffy said, turning a dark gaze on his father, only to have him meet it intrepidly. Duffy couldn't help but wonder what power of intimidation Maggie possessed that he didn't. "We've apparently been victims of a plot hatched by our fathers to force you and me together for as long as it took for us to…you know." He looked around him at the elegant surroundings. "This is a hotel. They've probably been here all this time, just waiting for us to announce our engagement or something." He frowned at his father again. "What did you do that morning we saw you off at the airport? Make a big circle and come right back and check into the hotel?"

He shook his head. "Elliott had already checked us in. I went home to get some clothes. We conceived the plan while waiting for you to bring Maggie home. She'd been lost and lonely and you're always so secure and in charge. You were made for each other. But we didn't know how you'd see that if you weren't forced together for a period of time sufficient to make you turn to each other."

"You should have trusted me," Duffy said. "I had my own agenda."

"So, did you?" Elliott asked Maggie.

"Did we what?"

"Turn to each other."

"Dad…I…you…!" She growled and turned in a circle, as though intent on escape but not sure which way to go. Duffy caught her arm, just in case.

"Tell them what happened," he advised, amusement overriding his mild annoyance with the two men.

She, however, had not come to that point. "I am not speaking to them!" she said, and tried to take off for the dining room.

He pulled her back and held her firmly beside him. "What does it matter who is responsible for the fact that we've spent the past two weeks together?"

She opened her mouth to offer an argument that it did matter, then looked into his eyes and seemed to lose her head of steam.

"They lied to us," she complained.

He nodded. "I know. We'll find a way to make them pay. Just tell them what happened."

Both men were now on their feet and looking worried.

"What happened?" Elliott asked.

Charlie pointed to his companion. "It was all his idea. He made me…"

Elliott backhanded him in the gut. "You weasel!" He turned his attention on his daughter. "What? What happened?"

"We're engaged," she said, then stiffly withstood their hugs and hoots of approval. Then she glared them into subsiding before her. "But don't think for one minute that we're inviting either of you to the wedding. Large gifts offered in an attempt to placate us can be left on the church steps."

"Of course." Charlie cleared his throat. "When is the wedding?"

"We were waiting for my father to return from overseas, where I was sure he was in mortal danger. Now he's simply in danger of me."

Elliott clapped Duffy on the shoulder. "Did you know about her temper?"

Duffy nodded. "I saw it a couple of times trying to get her to my place when she was determined to wait for you in Arlington. Thanks a lot for that, by the way."

Elliott smiled wryly, then tentatively took his daughter's hand. "So…I'm going to be a grandfather again?"

His eyes filled with tears at the prospect, and she seemed to have no choice but to let him wrap her in his arms.

Something clicked into place inside Duffy and gave him peace. Nothing more to worry about. Nothing at all.

Over dinner, the four of them set a wedding date for the weekend after the next. Then Duffy and Maggie drove home, and Elliott and Charlie, who'd enjoyed their days at the hotel, decided to stay until the wedding.

"Imagine them doing that to us!" Maggie grumbled to Duffy when he returned from seeing Judy home. "What on earth got into them?" The question was asked in a muffled tone as she pulled her dress over her head.

He grabbed her by her bare waist and dropped her onto his bed, pinning her there with a kiss at the base of her rib cage. Her muffled giggle came from inside the dress.

"I'd say inspiration got into them," he said, peeling off her stockings and panties.

Blinded by the yards of fabric that still ensnared her so that she couldn't see but only feel as he caught her knees and pulled her to him, she had to agree with him.

She'd never known such bliss, she thought that night, as they made love over and over. She'd loved Harry and her boys with all her heart, and the grief of losing them had heightened this rediscovery of life. It was as though someone had digitally remastered her life so that both color and sound were perfection.

It was so new and so wonderful that it was almost painful.

And it lasted until her agent called from London the following day.

"There you are!" Glen said when she answered the phone. "I thought I'd never track you down. I haven't even been able to find your father. What's up? It's not like you to go into hiding. Fortunately Baldy remembered that you were still with that Rambo-type security guy who rescued us with the gendarmes, or I'd still be looking for you. A call to his office got me this number."

"Hi, Glen." She was sunning on the beach and reading a novel while the boys and the Baker twins alternately chased each other and played in the sand with their toy cars and trucks. Duffy had gone to town to look at a shop for rent. "How are you?"

"Great!" he replied. "Priss and I spent a week and a half on the Riviera to recover from our ordeal, and now I have to go back to work to pay for her shopping. Hence, the reason for this call."

She smiled to herself, waiting for just the right moment to tell him her news.

"When are you coming home, anyway?" he asked.

She opened her mouth to tell him she wasn't—at least not permanently—when he forestalled her with, "You know Pierce Bachmeier?"

"Ah…well, I don't *know* him. I read for the part of Judith in *Woman in Peril* very early in my…"

"Okay, well apparently he's weary of America and wants to see how Europe reacts to his work."

Though a tyrant in production, Pierce wrote strong, complex characters and brilliant dialogue. "I'm sure Europe will embrace him. He's…"

"He wants you for the part of Caroline Carmody."

Maggie felt the world stop. Well, it didn't, of course. The ocean rolled on, the children ran and shouted, the sun toasted her with its warm brilliance, but she *felt* as though everything had stopped.

She sat up in surprise, the words sounding over and over in her ears, blotting out the rush of the surf.

Caroline   Carmody.   Caroline   Carmody.   Caroline Carmody.

"Mags?"

She heard Glen's voice, but she couldn't respond for the pointed lump of anguish in her throat. It was stupid to be upset, she told herself. Stupid to feel betrayed. She'd known the truth all along, after all. It was just Duffy who'd managed to convince her otherwise.

But now here was the simple truth, forced down her throat on a Trans-Atlantic telephone call.

Ten years ago she'd read for the part of Judith Carmody, and now she was being offered the part of Caroline—Judith's *fifty-two-year-old mother.*

Chapter Twelve

She knew her reaction was vain and ridiculous, but she didn't seem to be able to help herself. So much had happened to her in such a short amount of time. That was the only way she could explain the fantasy she'd fallen into, the belief that she could marry a man eight years her junior and mother his young children. She felt a sudden, overwhelming panic.

"Maggie!" Glen's voice said sharply. "Are you there?"

"I'm here, Glen," she replied finally, the dream receding as reality reasserted itself. And in line with a return to sanity was the need to resume the reins of her career. "When do you want me?"

"Can you be here day after tomorrow?"

The need to escape her near mistake was urgent. "Of course. But you know there's still two months on my contract with..."

"If that man of yours was able to get you a month's R and R, then I'm sure he and I can fix that, if you and Pierce decide you like each other."

"Duffy made him give me the break?" she asked. She'd suspected that originally, then forgotten about it when her life took a comfortable turn.

"Yes. He didn't want to, but March told him if he didn't, he'd regret it. Nonspecific threats seldom carry weight, unless the person making the threat looks like he's capable of anything. Anyway—your understudy's proven herself quite the professional and gotten good reviews. Besides, it may take him that long to put the package together. Want me to arrange for your flight?"

"Ah…" She felt a small pang as she got the image of herself flying away from here. In an instant the small pang grew to excruciating pain. She had to take charge. "Please, Glen. You'll meet me at Heathrow?"

"I will. And I'll tell Eponine you're coming home. Anxious to see you, Mags."

"You, too, Glen."

"Isn't it exciting to be launching a project again?"

The prospect of a new role had always been exciting to her. It stirred something inside her, made her eager to plumb her own depths for character substance and nuance. She sat still, waiting for that feeling.

It wasn't there.

She felt surprise and then panic, then realized that it couldn't possibly be there yet. She was reestablishing her hold on reality, but the influence of Duffy and his boys and Lamplight Harbor had been powerful. She'd actually believed she could live here, be happy here. It might take a while to regain her senses.

"Yes, it is," she lied to Glen. "You can fax me with my agenda." She gave him the number of Duffy's fax machine.

She sat with the boys for another hour while they played, pain becoming a firm fixture in her chest. It had to hurt, she told herself, to have a dream ripped out and replaced by reality.

Then Annie Baker, the twin's mother, appeared, plump and suntanned in shorts and wraparound shirt, to collect the twins for dinner.

"Congratulations, Maggie!" she said as she gathered the twins to her. "I'm so happy for Duffy! Well, for you, too, of course, but he has to be the best dad around. He deserves a good woman."

Maggie felt like Satan, herself, but smiled pleasantly and thanked her for her good wishes. Duffy could explain later.

When Annie walked away with the twins, Mike and Adam came to sit with Maggie, piling in between her knees all sandy and smelling of saltwater. She held them close, wondering how she could ever explain to them that she loved them like her very own children, but she had to go.

She was used up, and they deserved a young, happy mother who could fit into this wonderful place and be everything they and their father needed.

She was Caroline Carmody.

Maybe she'd get lucky, she thought selfishly, and Duffy would agree to explain it to them.

Once she explained it to him.

DUFFY THOUGHT something was wrong the moment he walked in the door. But he chided himself on this wariness he'd been living with since Maggie had agreed to marry him. Things weren't supposed to go this well for him. He'd been a business success from the day he opened March Security, and he had great friends and wonderful employees, but his personal life had always been a mess. He picked the wrong women, at first through inexperience, then through stupidity.

But he'd chosen well this time, so what could possibly account for this lingering sense of trouble waiting just above his head?

Music blared from the kitchen, for one thing. Usually when Maggie cooked, the boys fussed around her, talking her arm off, helping set the table or just sitting on the counter while she talked to them about acting, about England, about when she was a teenager and lived next door to their father.

They'd found it funny that he'd been younger than her and in a subordinate position. "You're bigger than Daddy!" Mike had said with a laugh.

He'd expected her to balk at that, but it had been the day after they'd made love and she'd laughed it off, a different woman than she'd been just the day before.

It had humbled him that loving him had driven away some of her concerns.

Instead of being in the kitchen with Maggie, the boys were sprawled on the floor, watching cartoons. Duffy leaned down to ruffle each head, his presence almost unnoticed as he stepped over them and went into the kitchen with the bottle of champagne he'd bought to celebrate his new furniture shop.

Maggie stood at the stove in white T-shirt, shorts and sandals, her short hair held away from her neck with a scissorlike clip. There was something on every burner, and she moved a wooden spoon from one pot to the other, poking and testing.

He wondered at her frantic preparations, when they'd made a point since she'd been here of simple meals that didn't require a lot of fuss and cleanup.

"Hi," he said, leaning down to plant a kiss on the side of her neck.

She started, as though he'd struck her. He straightened, an eyebrow raised in surprise.

"Sorry," she said with a quick, smiling glance at him. The smile was not at all sincere. Then the pots seemed to require her attention. "You scared me."

His plaguey inner fear took over. See? I told you it couldn't work out. She's a star, for God's sake, and you're nothing but muscle. Muscle with two little kids. What were you *thinking?*

Ignoring himself, he put the champagne in the refrigerator. "What's all this?" he asked.

"Baked chicken," she replied, "stuffing, mashed potatoes, carrots because Adam doesn't like peas, and peas because Mike doesn't like carrots. Baking powder biscuits for you."

Oh-oh. "Did you dent the Jeep?" he teased.

"You had the Jeep," she reminded him, clearly missing the joke.

"Max-out my credit card?"

"I got my own back last week, remember?"

"Then why are you working so hard?" he asked, deciding he was going to have to put the question straight to her. "Is there another man?" He was still teasing. He hoped.

She glanced up at him again with a look that stabbed him right in the heart. Not because it was cruel or guilty, but because it was chillingly detached. Her movements seemed nervous, calculated to keep her too busy to talk or listen, but her eyes said she had something to tell him that he was going to hate.

"Have you ever heard of Pierce Bachmeier?" she asked. She took the bubbling potatoes off the stove and poured them into a colander. Steam wafted up.

"No," he replied. She walked around him to reach the salt and butter she'd put on the counter. He knew he was planted squarely in her way, but he wasn't leaving until he understood what was going on.

"He's a brilliant playwright," she said, "and he's taking one of his plays to Europe."

He could guess the rest, and felt relief at the knowledge that that wouldn't be a problem for him.

"And he wants you?" he asked, handing her the measuring cup of milk when she pointed to it. "Smart man. We can work that out. The logistics might get tricky, but…"

"He wants me to play a character named Caroline

Carmody.'' She poured the potatoes back into the pan, added salt, butter and milk and began to mash. ''It's a role with great range and complexity. I'm…I'm…excited.''

''Of course,'' he said, something in her manner scaring him. He talked on, hoping it wasn't obvious. ''I thought your decision to quit the stage needed a second look. We can—''

''No, we can't,'' she said firmly, though she didn't raise her voice. She stopped mashing and drew a deep breath.

His panic level reached the red zone.

''What are you saying, Maggie?'' he asked.

She started mashing again. ''I'm saying that it was all just a summer-in-Maine fantasy, Duffy. Waterfront cottages, lobster pots, antique shops, bakeries and churches with white steeples!'' Every highlight seemed to deserve a particularly violent mash. ''Who wouldn't fall for that and believe it was the end of the rainbow? And Lamplight Harbor? Who couldn't imagine living to old age on the front porch of a beach house in a place called Lamplight Harbor?'' She was now angry, and he wasn't sure why.

He leaned a hip on the counter and folded his arms. ''Well, not you, apparently,'' he said. ''Is that what you're trying to tell me?''

''I'm trying to tell you it isn't real!'' she said, planting the masher in the potatoes with a smack and holding it there while she glared at him. ''I told you it was impossible, but you got me all wrapped up in this perfect little world and I…I *believed* you!''

He didn't want to be angry, as well. He fought a rising temper with all the self-control he had.

"Maggie, if you want to go back to the stage, I understand," he said patiently. "I don't *want* you to quit for us. The boys love you. As long as they can be part of your life, it doesn't matter if you have to—"

"That's not what I'm talking about!"

"Then what the hell *are* you talking about?"

"I mean," she said, resuming her mashing, "that I can't marry you, Duffy. I was crazy to think I could. And so were you."

"Why?" he asked baldly.

She made a rapid, hands-outstretched gesture that he guessed was supposed to say it was beyond explanation, then went back to mashing with a shake of her head.

He snatched the masher from her and tossed it in the sink.

"Why?" he repeated. "What's changed since this morning?" She'd awakened him with kisses and laughter, and they'd made love before breakfast.

"I just thought it through," she said, avoiding his eyes by playing with the salt shaker. "And I decided that this was just a summer..." She was speaking slowly and finally stopped altogether when forced to explain what it had been. "A summer thing," she said finally.

He guessed it was the deliberately careless and unfocused nature of the word that snapped his tenuous hold on temper.

"Thing?" he repeated, his voice quiet and cold while inside a fire raged. His voice rose in volume as he went on. "You stand me on my head, delude the boys into thinking they have a mother, and you call it a *thing*? And a *summer thing*? As though it comes and goes with the phases of the moon?!"

She looked startled by his reaction. "Duffy..."

"What made you decide to 'think it through'?" he demanded, judging by the way she avoided his eyes that there was more to it. "Just a brief eight hours ago you weren't thinking about anything but what it was like to be in my arms."

She angled her chin and said haughtily, "Well, we won't be spending all our lives in bed, will we?"

"Oh, as though that's all I care about!" he shouted with impatience. "I want to know what happened."

She folded her arms stubbornly. "Don't yell at me."

He drew a breath and made one more effort to rein in his anger. "Start making sense," he suggested, "and I'll stop yelling."

She walked around him to turn off the carrots and the peas, then turned the oven down to warm. She put a hand to her forehead, and he noticed that it trembled. It was a relief for him to see that because it suggested she did care, despite this sudden change of heart. She looked both vulnerable and miserable. He pulled a chair out from the table and pushed her into it.

"Tell me," he said.

Tears brimmed in her eyes. He waited patiently, fighting himself to understand her.

"Glen called," she said, her voice quiet but strained. "Pierce wants me to come to London."

He nodded. He'd already explained to her that that wasn't a problem for him. What he didn't understand was why it was a problem for her.

"He wants me to play Caroline Carmody," she said, as though he should understand what that meant.

"Right." He repeated what she'd told him. "It's a strong, complex role. You said that."

Her eyes met his, sad and wounded. "She's fifty-two," she said.

For a moment he still didn't get the significance of that.

"Fifty-two," he repeated. And as he said the words—the *age*—he realized what it meant. His immediate inclination was to laugh at the absurdity of that, then he remembered that the offer of that role and her reaction to it was destroying his world. And he lost his last effort to restrain himself.

"You're telling me," he asked, everything inside him pulsing with anger, "that this is an age problem? That because you're a great actress and you've been asked to play an older woman, your feelings are hurt?" His voice was rising in volume. He couldn't help himself. Oh, hell, he didn't want to. He'd finally had it.

She looked disappointed in his assessment. "It

goes deeper than that, Duffy. It's more a case of finally realizing I was deluding myself.''

He rolled his eyes and paced away from her for fear of what he'd do if he stayed too close. "So you're deciding *our* future in the real world based on what's going on *on the stage?*"

"The stage is *my* real world!" she shouted at him. "And if any venue in the world does age-appropriate casting, it's the theater. I'm almost forty and apparently I'm starting to look it. I can't pretend that isn't true.''

He was so exasperated with her, he could barely string words together. "That's so ridiculous. You're willing to sacrifice our future, my children's future, for the sake of your vanity?''

"It's not vanity!" she screamed at him. "The boys need a lively, spirited mother, not one who's going to get creaky before they're teenagers! You're only thirty-one. You should have some sassy young thing with the whole world ahead of her.''

There was a look in her eyes he'd seen the night he'd stayed with her in London. It was a mix of grief and hopelessness, and he finally understood what this was all about.

He came back to the table and stood over her, knowing that even if he understood what motivated her, this was no time to be merciful.

"I think that this has nothing to do with age," he said. "I think it's just another handy excuse so you don't have to get entangled with a family all over again. It's a hell of a lot of trouble, and for two years all you've had to do is work, collect applause and money and party across Europe with your high-living friends. I think you realize that you and I have the potential to be as happy as you and Harry were, that you'd be able to love my boys as much as you loved your own, and you're afraid of that. So you're retreating.''

Maggie bristled and stood, prepared to do battle. How dare he reduce her complicated emotions to selfishness and the need to party. She opened her mouth to rebut his accusations, but he stopped her with a raised hand.

''Never mind,'' he said wearily. ''If this is going to keep coming up, then you're right. You can't marry me.''

A moment ago she'd wanted desperately for him to see that. Now that he not only saw but agreed, she felt as though she were sinking in quicksand and the world was disappearing as the sand sucked her in.

''The boys,'' he went on, ''deserve a mother who's anxious to be with them, not someone who keeps finding excuses to run away. And, frankly, I'm not sure how long I'd be able to take the weird heaven-and-hell thing we've got going here. You make love to me at night like a madwoman, then you look at me in the light of day as though you've never seen me before.''

He put his cup on the counter and sighed, suddenly coolly detached. ''When are you leaving?''

The question was so chillingly to the point that she needed a moment to reply.

"Glen's making my arrangements," she said, her voice flat. "I'm supposed to be in London day after tomorrow."

"Ah. Then probably tomorrow sometime."

"I think so."

"I'd like you to explain it to Mike and Adam."

Of course. It was her responsibility. "I will."

"Then, I guess you and I have nothing more to say to each other." He walked to the doorway, then stopped and turned. "Except…what happened to that gutsy sixteen-year-old girl who picked up a handful of fire and walked out of my room with it?"

"I was younger then," she replied.

He nodded. "And braver," he added, and left the room.

HER ITINERARY was very straightforward. New York to London at 8:02 a.m. tomorrow. She'd called her father, explained quickly about her trip and side-stepped his surprised questions with the simple information that it was complicated and she didn't want to talk about it. However, if he'd like to accompany her to London, she'd be happy to host him for as long as he wanted to stay, since his connivance had prevented her from seeing much of him since she'd been in Maine.

He agreed, then after a brief conversation with Charlie March, told her he and Charlie would pick her up at 5:30 tomorrow morning, and Charlie would fly them from the small airfield at Owl's Head to Kennedy Airport.

She'd packed, now all she had to do was tuck the boys in and explain that she was leaving. Duffy had brought them upstairs after a wild wrestling match on the living room floor to wear them out and soften them up.

She was so miserable she could hardly breathe. She sat on the edge of her bed beside the bag she'd just closed and locked, and tried to find words.

Duffy stuck his head in her room. "They're waiting for you in Mike's room," he said, then he stepped aside.

Knowing it wouldn't help to delay, she went right into Mike's room where both boys sat propped against the pillows. She remembered the night they'd been missing, how they'd sat together in this bed afterward, upset because their father had been so angry and gaining comfort in each other. She'd been able to make sense to them then; she was sure she could do it again.

But that time she'd explained love, not betrayal.

It wasn't betrayal, she told herself as she smiled at them, it was…it was protection. She was saving them for a younger, more wonderful mother.

She could tell by their faces that Duffy had done something to prepare them. They looked distressed and uncertain.

Mike, who never backed around an issue, said directly, "Dad says you have to go away."

"That's right," she said, feeling even worse that though Duffy had insisted he was going to leave the dirty job to her, he'd tried to help her. "I have another job and I have to go back to London."

"And you're not gonna be our mom."

"No," she said, wrapping her arms around both blanket-clad pairs of knees. "But you can come and see me in—"

Mike shook his head. "It's okay. Our other mother didn't like us, either." He had a look of grim acceptance no child should have to feel.

"I'm sure that wasn't it," Maggie said quickly. "I'm sure she loved you, but she knew your dad would do a better job of being your parent than she would."

Mike didn't seem to get that. "But a dad can't be a mom."

How did she answer that? Sometimes you can't have both? Didn't every child have a right to both if it was at all possible? Yes, but if he had a mother, he had the right to a young one eager to be everything to him.

"And not every woman can be a mom," she said, catching two little hands. "I've come to love both of you very much, but I don't think I'd do a good job of being your mom. I work a lot and—" And what? I'm still heartbroken? I feel old and over with? I'm afraid?

Mike nodded. "It's okay. Dad said you love us, but you still love your boys that died and that you'll always be sad about that. And it's hard to love somebody when you're sad. I mean, you can *feel* it, but it's hard to *do* it."

Oh, he did, did he? And what made him think he understood everything?

"So, next summer," she said, trying to draw herself out of that quicksand pit and generate a more cheerful note, "I want the two of you to come and see me in London. I'll send you tickets for the plane, and we'll do all kinds of really fun things. Will you come?"

Mike smiled feebly. "Sure."

Adam nodded. "But, can't Daddy come?"

Mike rolled his eyes at him. "No, he can't come, 'cause they had a fight and they don't love each other anymore. That's why she's leaving." He smiled at her quickly. "Dad didn't say that. I figured it out. I heard you yelling in the kitchen."

She leaned down to wrap her arms around them. "I want you to promise me that you'll be good for your dad, that you won't take off without telling him ever again and that you'll work hard in school. Okay? 'Cause you're both very smart, and if you work hard, you'll have a very happy life. And I'd really like to know that you were happy."

Mike hugged her fiercely. "Okay."

Adam looked confused. "I'd be happy without all that if you were here."

Mike elbowed him.

"Okay," he said dutifully.

She kissed each of them, then turned out their light. She couldn't see her way across the hall for the tears in her eyes. She closed her door behind her as sobs erupted in her throat. She changed into a

cotton nightshirt, pulled on the sweater Duffy had
given her the night he'd rescued them, then curled
into a ball in the middle of her bed and cried herself
to sleep.

Chapter Thirteen

On the surface the goodbye was easy. Duffy had considered waking her during the night with a whole new list of arguments on why she should stay, or how he and the boys could accompany her if she chose to go, but then he reminded himself that he'd done all that and she'd still been determined.

Then he'd considered staying in bed so that he didn't have to wave her off when his father drove her and Elliott to the airport, but that would have been cowardly, and being a shield to the world was his business.

When he decided he had to see her off, he wanted to be cool and detached, but then he got up when he heard her stirring and went to close the door to Mike's room where Adam had spent the night and intercepted her in the hallway. She was disheveled and red-eyed and wearing his black sweater. She looked both joyful and horrified to see him.

Whatever detachment he'd thought he could muster dissolved completely, and he'd have taken her in his arms if it wouldn't have just made it that much more difficult for both of them.

"Good morning," he said, and tried to give her an honest smile. But it wasn't much of one. "I'm making coffee and an omelette so you'll have something in your stomach for the drive."

She swallowed before she answered. "Thank you," she whispered.

"Sure."

They ate in silence, their fathers arrived, and it was all suddenly that much more horrible because of the forced joviality of the men who loved both of them so much that they'd concocted an elaborate scheme to get them together.

Elliott helped Duffy carry her things out to the car, then as Maggie directed the arrangement of them in the trunk, Charlie came to clap Duffy on the shoulder.

"Is it all right if I come back to spend the night?" he asked. "I'll make dinner."

His father guessed he was going to need him. "Sure," he said, putting an arm around his shoulders. "Thanks."

Then he was climbing into the car, Elliott waved from over the top of it, his eyes grim, his mouth moving uncertainly as he got into the back.

And Duffy was alone on the sidewalk with Maggie.

He searched his mind for something profound to say, but it wasn't operating this morning. It didn't matter, anyway, because she threw her arms around him, held him tightly for one torturous moment, then she was getting into the car. His father tapped the horn and drove away.

CHARLIE WAS BACK well before lunch. The Bakers had stopped by and invited the boys to join them on a fishing outing, and Duffy had happily let them go, knowing it would be good for them to be distracted and good for him to be alone. He couldn't remember ever feeling this badly.

His father, however, seemed determined to talk. "I think she'll come back, given time," he said after Duffy explained what had happened. "You've never lost a mate or a child. I mean, Lisa left but that's not really the same thing. It's been two years since the train accident, but a person can't just put all those memories aside to make new ones until they're ready. And she's obviously not ready."

He understood that. He remembered clearly how he'd felt when he hadn't known where his boys were for several long hours. He couldn't imagine how he'd feel knowing they were gone—forever. But that understanding didn't ease his sense of loss or help him make his boys understand it.

And somehow knowing she was entitled to her grief and confusion only made his own sadness worse. There wasn't even anything he could do about it.

"Want to go to the country club and hit some balls?" Charlie asked.

"No, thanks," Duffy replied.

"Movie?

"No."

"Walk to the bakery?"

"Thanks, but maybe I'll just spend some time in my shop. Now that I've rented a space, I've got to produce something."

Charlie looked doubtful about that decision. "You think you should be using power tools in your state of mind?"

Duffy smiled reluctantly. "You afraid I'll dremel myself to death?"

"No, but that staple thing's a mean so and so."

"I'll be fine, Dad. Come along if you want. I'll give you something to sand."

"I'm glad you're giving up the security business," his father said, following him into the shop. Duffy flipped the switch, the fluorescents flickered, then filled the cool room with light.

It took him a minute to remember that he'd never shared that plan with his father.

"Maggie told me," Charlie explained when he turned to him in surprise. "She didn't realize I didn't know."

Duffy didn't care that she'd told him. It just hurt to hear her name.

"It'll be good for the boys to have you around more," Charlie went on. "And this is such a great place to be year-round. I might even consider selling the house and coming here."

Duffy settled him in an old captain's chair. "What

would Elliott do without you? You've been neighbors for so long.''

''He's thinking of moving to London to be with Maggie.'' He sighed and pulled his reading glasses out of his shirt pocket as Duffy handed him an intricately carved spindle from an old chair. ''He's really worried about her.''

Duffy liked the thought of Elliott being nearby if Maggie needed him. They were probably sitting side by side in first-class seats right now somewhere over the Atlantic.

He closed his eyes and imagined her in his arms.

Imagination was all he had now.

''MARGARET EMMALINE LAWTON,'' Elliott said firmly, ''if you don't stop pacing and decide whether or not we're going to London, I'm going to leave you alone in this airport and go *home!*''

She glanced at him as she continued to pace. Travelers in the terminal at Kennedy hurried by them, and a small child with Mickey Mouse ears and a balloon watched them with interest.

''Don't get high-handed with me, Dad,'' Maggie said. ''You're the one who got me into this mess.'' She gave him a speaking look. ''And we wouldn't want you to have another *attack,* would we?''

''*I* made you decide not to get on your flight because you changed your mind three times about whether or not to go back to Duffy?'' he asked, ignoring her reference to the ruse he'd used to make her come home.

"No," she replied distractedly, remembering that coming home had been rather wonderful, all in all. "You made me stay with him, which made me fall in love with him when I'm not ready to love another man and his children."

"What do you mean, 'not ready'?" he asked, looking up at her as she paced by him. "Being chicken and not being ready are not the same thing."

"Maybe I'm chicken *because* I'm not ready."

"No, you're chicken because Harry was cerebral and took care of you, but Duffy's smart but passionate and considers you an equal. He's going to expect you to do your part, not simply be an object of adoration. That's going to be different for you."

She stopped in shock to stare at him. "I've never just been…"

He forestalled her with a nod. "I know, sweetheart. But Harry perceived you as a star. Duffy sees you as a flesh-and-blood woman."

"Daddy." She sank down beside him on the black vinyl seat and put a hand to her aching head. "I'm older than he is. The boys are young and lively and…"

"Maggie," he said, putting an arm around her shoulders and squeezing her to him. "You are young, you've just been concentrating on death for so long you've forgotten what it's like to be alive. I thought Duffy and his boys had reminded you, but your happiness there apparently didn't take."

"I've been offered the role of a fifty-two-year-old woman, Dad!"

"Because you're a good actress!"

"Yeah? Well, I get that from you," she retorted with sarcasm.

"I wasn't acting." He squared his shoulders, finally reacting to her accusations. "I did have a brief…spell. But it was indigestion."

Maggie got to her feet, hugged him, then dug into her purse for her calling card and drew a breath.

"I am a good actress," she said firmly. "That's what I've done well, and that's what I'm going to continue to do—even if I have to play an old woman. I'm going to call Glen and tell him we've been delayed, but we're on our way. I just got…emotional, that's all. I know I'm doing the right thing by leaving them so they can find another mom, another…lover. I had the courage to make that decision once. I can't welch on it now. Sit tight, I'll bring us back a mocha."

"Maggie…"

"Be right back, Dad."

Glen sounded happy to hear her voice. "Are you on the plane?" he asked.

"No," she said, fanning herself with her card. "I missed it. But I'll be there."

"Great. Listen, Pierce's here. Want to say hi?"

"Ah…sure."

Pierce's big, booming voice came over the line as though he stood in front of her. "I'm so glad you're coming, Maggie," he said. "This is going to be a brilliant production. I'm very excited about it."

She diplomatically agreed that it would. "I hope

my crow's feet don't show to the audience," she
teased.

There was a moment's pause. "Pardon me?" he
said.

"My crow's feet," she explained. "Actresses are
vain, Pierce. You're asking me to play a woman in
her fifties when I'm just turning forty. You have to
expect me to harass you about it a little bit."

"Well...Maggie. Did you think I was redoing
Woman in Peril?" he asked. She heard him cover
the mouthpiece and say something to Glen, who
laughed uproariously.

"Aren't you?"

"No." Now he was laughing. "Crow's feet in-
deed. I've written a prequel to that called *Woman in
Love.* It's about Caroline's rise to prominence in
fashion and her affair with a judge. It spans five
years. She's twenty-nine to thirty-four. You should
feel complimented not insulted."

Again the world stopped. The child with the
mouse-ears hat walked away, a plane sped down the
runway, her watch ticked. She felt suddenly as
though every cell in her body had regenerated itself.

"Twenty-nine?" she asked incredulously after a
long pause.

"Twenty-nine," he confirmed.

She stared at the mouthpiece on the phone and
wondered if she'd lost her mind.

IT WAS ONLY EIGHT O'CLOCK, but Charlie was already yawning. The boys had come home exhausted

and had eaten dinner and gone to bed. The house was painfully quiet, no humming from the kitchen where Maggie cleaned up or baked, no CD player going with music, no Maggie reclining on the sofa with the evening paper or a magazine.

God. She'd been gone less than a day and he was already feeling as though it had been months. He tried to imagine where she was. Glen was meeting her at the airport and had probably taken her to some exclusive restaurant for dinner. They would be talking business by now. He wondered if she was laughing at Glen's jokes, or if she was thinking of him and Lamplight Harbor and remembering the night they'd first made love.

A large, dark emptiness opened right in the center of his being. Deciding that would never do, he got up and headed for the kitchen to make a pot of decaf and see if there were any doughnuts left from his father's afternoon excursion to town.

When he walked in and saw Maggie and Elliott standing there, he thought he'd gone over the edge.

Maggie was wearing the jeans and short red top she'd left in that morning, and looked as though she'd been crying. Elliott looked a lot like he had the day Charlie had flown him in to tell him about Maggie's kidnap.

"What happened?" Duffy asked anxiously.

She was studying his face, clearly trying to read what he was thinking. But since he had no clue what was happening, he didn't know what to think.

"I'm back," she said unnecessarily. She took a

step toward him. She looked terrified and yet curiously free. He grew more confused. He wanted to reach for her, but he didn't think he'd have the guts to let her go again.

She opened her mouth, seemingly ready to say more, then closed it again and hurried around him and up the stairs.

"Maggie!" he heard his father say in the living room. Then he appeared beside him and embraced his friend, who looked relieved and happy to see him.

"We are never acting as Cupids again!" Elliott said. "I've driven up and down the coast, I've been to the airport and not gone anywhere, and I've spent hours in the car with a weeping woman. I tell you, I've had it!"

Charlie tried to comfort him. "Well, fortunately, they're the only kids we've got, so this isn't likely to come up again. What are you doing home?"

"Frankly," Elliott said, "I don't know. I just know that I'm exhausted and I need a beer. Can you drive?"

"Of course."

Elliott went to Duffy and gave him a bear hug. "Duff, all I can ask is that you hear her out and remember that women's minds are wired differently from ours. And that love can be perverse, confused, complex, even painful, but it's still love and should be respected as such. You know what I mean?"

"No," Duffy said candidly.

"Good," Elliott replied. "I'd worry about you if you did. Come on, Charlie. I really need that beer."

They hurried off, and Duffy was left to stand alone in his kitchen and wonder what in the hell was going on. It occurred to him that he'd done that often since Maggie had walked back into his life. Or he'd walked into hers.

He made the coffee as he'd intended and was reaching for cups when she appeared in the kitchen doorway.

"Hi," she said, absurdly.

"Hi," he replied. He was feeling a little absurd, himself.

"I wanted to tuck them in." She pointed over her head, indicating, he guessed, Mike and Adam. "But they were both fast asleep. So I just watched them sleep."

He went to the fridge for the cream she liked in her coffee. "You're not going to be able to fly back from London every night to do that, you know."

"I didn't go," she said. "I changed my mind so many times about coming back that we missed our first flight, then I booked another flight and changed my mind again."

"You seemed pretty sure what you were doing when you left."

"I thought I was. I thought leaving you would be best for you."

He gave her a look that suggested how ridiculous he thought that was, but made no move toward her. He had to keep his distance until he knew why she was back.

She looked sheepish for a moment, then squared

her shoulders and met his gaze. "I know. I was really thinking about what was best for me. Acting allows me to be someone else, and I can't do that here. I thought I didn't want to be me because that woman hurts and sometimes feels old. And the offer of that role exaggerated everything I felt."

"Insane," he said, leaning against the counter, "when you wear those tiny jeans and there isn't a line on your face."

She took the compliment with a small smile, and he noticed that there was something buoyant in it. Hope swelled in him, but he was afraid to trust it.

"Thank you."

"Don't thank me," he said. "I was just going to add that you also act like a spoiled child. Nothing mature about that."

She hitched a shoulder up, accepting the jibe. "You're absolutely right. Then I called Glen's office to tell him I was coming, after all, and Pierce was there."

He remained still, waiting for enlightenment.

"Seems the play he wanted to cast me in was a *prequel* to the play I knew," she said, watching him warily. "My character ages from twenty-nine to thirty-four in it."

Damn it. That seemed to resolve things for her but not for him. He felt a bitter and painful disappointment.

"Is that why you're back?" he asked. "Because you're not being cast as an older woman after all? Because that somehow soothes your ego and makes you believe that I want you back because you'll be taking center stage as a woman younger than your age rather than as one older?''

''No.''

It was all he could do to hold his ground as she came toward him and put her hands on his chest. He didn't want to make contact because then he wouldn't be able to make a sensible decision here. And he had two little boys to think about.

''I'm back because I turned him down. I'd be lying if I said it didn't make me feel less matronly to know the role was for a younger woman. Mostly, the closer I got to all that had once meant so much to me, I realized it no longer mattered. I think I held on to the age issue because it allowed me to hold on to the grief. They seemed to go together. And when I saw a whole new life taking shape around me—a life I wasn't sure I was equipped for anymore—I got scared. I wanted to go back where I could be some-body else.''

That was all hopeful, and he fell for it hook, line and sinker. But he had to *know* for certain before he could tell his boys in the morning that Maggie was back.

''And how do I know you won't wake up tomor-row and want to leave all over again?''

In answer, she wrapped her arms around him, stood on tiptoe and kissed him with convincing fer-vor. He even thought he felt something new in it, something…permanent.

But he caught her by the arms and pulled her away, holding her a small distance from him.

Maggie felt something inside her cave in on itself. She'd cried and chattered all the way home, trying to imagine how Duffy would react to her return, discussing her explanation with her father, getting dos-and-don'ts advice.

But that thunderous expression on Duffy's face made it pretty clear she'd failed.

"I like the kiss," he said, "but I want to hear it in words."

It felt too big for words, but she prayed to be inspired with the right ones.

"I guess," she began hesitantly, "that, though I was gone from you only one day, it felt like the lighting was off in my life or the script was bad. I need you. I need you to need me." Something softened in his eyes at that and, encouraged, she kept talking.

"I love you, Duffy. I think I have since you showed up that night in the Pyrenees. But I had sedated myself emotionally, and falling in love with you meant emotions rehab."

A smile twitched at his lips. "You're mixing metaphors."

"But am I convincing enough?"

"You're very close."

She thought she knew what would put her over. "Okay," she said. "You wait right here." She got to the door, then turned and said quickly, "I'm not changing my mind. I just left something in the car."

"Our dads left with the car."

"Oh, no!" She yanked the door open, intending to check to be sure, when Elliott and Charlie fell into the kitchen.

Duffy came toward them with a frown he was having difficulty maintaining. "I thought you were out of the Cupid business."

"Yeah, well, we've got a vested interest in how this comes out." Elliott brushed Charlie off as they helped each other to their feet.

Maggie rushed out to the van to get the box she'd left in the back. She carried it carefully back to the kitchen, deposited it in the middle of the floor and unlatched the little gate at the side.

Duffy watched in surprise as a golden retriever puppy walked out on giant feet. He was about eight weeks old, fat and the color of clover honey. He had large brown eyes, curly, floppy ears, and as Duffy squatted down for a closer look, he scampered to him and leaped up to kiss his face as though he'd been trained to ingratiate himself.

"A puppy!" Adam screeched from the doorway. "Look, Mike! A puppy? Dad! Is it our puppy? Huh? Dad?"

Mike joined Adam on the floor and looked up at Duffy in disbelief. "Adam woke me up. He said he thought he heard Maggie's voice." Then he saw Maggie, and his mouth fell open farther.

She got on her knees to hug him. Adam saw nothing but the puppy, but she assured him that it belonged to him and Mike.

"What do you think about calling her Lamplight?" she straightened to ask Duffy.

His eyes ran over her face, love bright in them. "Depends," he said. "What do you think about calling you Maggie March?"

She wrapped her arms around him. "I do," she replied.

The puppy squirmed excitedly, its wagging tail swatting a giggling Adam's face.

"You know you're going to end up feeding her," Duffy said to Maggie as he wrapped both arms around her from behind.

She leaned her head back against him. "Oh, sure."

"You'll have to help me build a dog run."

"Okay."

"And she'll need long walks on the beach."

She sighed and squeezed his arms. "So will I, or I'll get fat and lazy in my contentment."

He kissed the side of her throat. "I'll chase you around a lot to help keep you in shape."

"That's my boy!" Charlie said, pushing the back door open again. "Always self-sacrificing. Would one or both of you like to commend us now on our matchmaking skills?" He smiled at Elliott and both waited ingenuously for praise.

Maggie unwrapped herself from Duffy's embrace and went to hug Charlie. "Thank you for throwing us together," she said, then moving to her own father, hugged him and added, "and thank you, Dad, for all those lying, cheating things you taught me were unacceptable behavior.''

The men looked at one another, aware they were being chastised as well as thanked.

"You were being stubborn," Elliott said. "Desperate measures were required."

"Thank you," she said sincerely, "but now that you're going to be a grandfather again, I'd go easy on the creative manipulations, okay?"

"Okay."

Duffy came to join them and the four stood arm in arm, watching the boys and puppy at play.

Maggie turned to Duffy and looked into his eyes, enclosing the two of them in an adoring moment. "Thank you," she whispered, "for making me real again."

He leaned closer to give her a brief kiss. "Thank you," he replied, "for making my dreams real."

"Wow!" Mike, the puppy slurping kisses up and down his face, turned away in high giggle to focus on his family. The puppy turned his attention to Adam, who fell onto his back on the floor, laughing hysterically. "Maggie's just learning to be a mom and already she's the best one ever!"

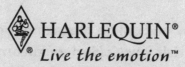

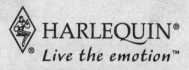

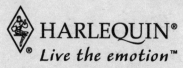

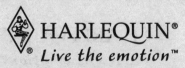

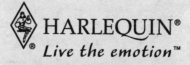

HARLEQUIN®

AMERICAN *Romance*®

Celebrating 20 Years
of home, heart and happiness!

As part of our yearlong 20th Anniversary celebration, Harlequin American Romance is launching a brand-new cover look this April. And, in the coming months, we'll be bringing back some of your favorite authors and miniseries. Don't miss:

THAT SUMMER IN MAINE
by Muriel Jensen

A heartwarming story of unexpected second chances, available in April 2003.

SAVED BY A TEXAS-SIZED WEDDING
by Judy Christenberry

Another story in Judy's bestselling *Tots for Texans* series, available in May 2003.

TAKING OVER THE TYCOON
by Cathy Gillen Thacker

A spin-off story from Cathy's series, *The Deveraux Legacy*, available in June 2003.

We've got a stellar lineup for you all year long, so join in the celebration and enjoy all Harlequin American Romance has to offer.

Available at your favorite retail outlet.

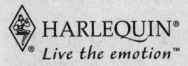

HARLEQUIN®
Live the emotion™

Visit us at www.eHarlequin.com

HARTAC2